HEART SISTER

HEART SISTER

MICHAEL F. STEWART

ORCA BOOK PUBLISHERS

Published in Canada and the United States in 2020 by Orca Book Publishers.
orcabook.com

Library and Archives Canada Cataloguing in Publication
Title: Heart sister / Michael F. Stewart.
Names: Stewart, Michael F., author.
Identifiers: Canadiana (print) 20200184601 | Canadiana (ebook) 2020018461x |
ISBN 9781459824874 (softcover) | ISBN 9781459824881 (PDF) | ISBN 9781459824898 (EPUB)
Classification: LCC PS8637.T49467 H43 2020 | DDC jc813/.6—dc23

Library of Congress Control Number: 2020930594

Summary: After his twin sister's death, a teenage filmmaker
tries to track down the recipients of her organs in hopes that it
will help his parents move on from the loss of their daughter.

Orca Book Publishers is committed to reducing the consumption
of nonrenewable resources in the making of our books. We make
every effort to use materials that support a sustainable future.

Orca Book Publishers gratefully acknowledges the support for its
publishing programs provided by the following agencies: the Government
of Canada, the Canada Council for the Arts and the Province of British Columbia
through the BC Arts Council and the Book Publishing Tax Credit.

Edited by Tanya Trafford
Cover images by Katie Carey
Cover design by Rachel Page
Typeset by Ella Collier
Author photo by Natasha Stewart

Printed and bound in Canada.

23 22 21 20 • 1 2 3 4

For my brother's heart sister and her family.

Dear Heart Family,

Inside me beats your daughter's heart. I am not allowed to tell you very much about myself. I would if I could. What I can tell you is that I am your heart daughter. If she had a sibling, then "Hiya, Heart bro or sis," *waves* I am your heart sister. I will do everything I can to hold her close.

It makes me so sad to know I only live because of another's death. But I'm not just alive because of her—I am born. I have never really lived, not yet, and your daughter's heart is giving me a chance to begin.

Ever since I was a baby, I was protected because of my bad heart. Protected from exercise. Protected from even crying too hard. I came home early. Never learned to ride a bike or to swim. What if I fell off? What if I went too far? My only adventures came in books. And I didn't dare to dream.

Now? Now I have a heart that can keep up with my dreams. I dream of climbing mountains. I dream of crossing oceans. Your daughter and me, we'll adventure together.

I promise to be amazing, just like I know your daughter must have been. I want so much to know all about her.

Please write.

ONE

Six weeks following my sister's death, I find her heart's location.

There's an envelope on my mother's dresser from the National Transplant Organization. Inside is a letter written in flowing script and pink ink.

"When did this come?" I ask my mom, wandering back through the kitchen with the letter and the reading glasses I'd gone searching for. I hesitate. *Is she ready for this?* She's been on bereavement leave since the accident, but I don't think her lying around all day is normal. Tissues litter a coffee table cluttered with cups of unfinished tea. Blinds let slip a thin ladder of light across the far wall. Plants droop at the windowsill.

I turn the lights on, awakening the room.

My mom waves me off from where she's stretched out on the couch, staring at a daytime game show and patting our dog, Sirius, with slow strokes, his marble eyes unblinking. I'm expecting more from her, but I don't know why.

"This is a letter from the person who received Minnie's heart!"

"For one thousand dollars…what pyramid retains a limestone cap?" the television host interjects.

"Have you even read it?" I ask.

She winces, drawing her knees to her chest and curling into a fetal position. Quick, sharp breaths whistle out from her and then the spasm ends. She unfolds. I shut the lights back off.

My sister would have known what to say. She finished half of my sentences. She'd have known what to do. I find myself looking around for her, even though I know she's gone.

My mom nods but ignores the letter, just as she ignores the glasses she asked me to find that I set on the sofa arm.

I gotta get her off the couch.

"Mom, you can't just…" I jerk a thumb at the television. She clutches the remote to her chest.

The post date on the envelope says the letter was sent two weeks ago. It occurs to me that there might be more. I jog to the front door and open it to a cool-for-August day. Across the street a neighbor nods uncertainly at me as he sweeps his porch. The tightly packed, identical townhouses seem to lean away from ours. They are all somehow more colorful than ours with its bruised siding.

A dead squirrel lies twisted in the middle of the street, and I think I've got to tell Minnie about it. But then I remember. Again.

The mailbox is stuffed with several envelopes and a couple of community newspapers. I gather it all up and head back into the house. I dump the pile on the dark burl of the dining room table and sort through it. I spot another envelope with the same transplant-organization logo.

Now, guessing what could be inside, I wonder if I should open it. Who wrote it? Who else has my twin sister inside them? What if I hate them? It feels a little like I'm picking at the scabs of Minnie's death. But wouldn't knowing more about the people Minnie has saved help my mom find a way to feel that her daughter lives on? I need to be strong for her. Maybe I can decide if it's something she should see.

I slip a fingernail along the edge and carefully pry open the seal.

Hi!

> *Thanks for the corneas. The transplanters won't let me say anything personal. Nothing that will allow you to draw any connections to me. I am a man who couldn't see. And now I can. Thanks. It means a bunch.*
> *See you. Off to catch butterflies.*

A small child has scrawled a butterfly and a crayon-lettered note in the corner.

Grandpa helps me ride my bike.

The note is signed with an eyeball beside the butterfly.

I look at the envelope again. The return address is the transplant organization's. Someone there functions as a go-between. But I grin at the note, because they missed something.

To me, this writer is asking to be found. He highlighted the rules and then gave me a personal clue. I'd give anything to have another minute with my sister. Even just a small part of her.

"Mom, check this out," I say, waggling the note. "It's from the guy who received Minnie's eyes." I stand in the doorway to the living room and wait for her response. The game-show host drones on. The refrigerator compressor rattles to life. It sounds an awful lot like a hospital room.

If my mother hears me, she gives no sign. Like she has every day since Minnie's death, she just lies there, cradling the remote control and patting Sirius. Patches of his fur have been loved away.

She's worse in the mornings. By the afternoon she usually gets up to brush her teeth, at least. But I've noticed she's been getting off the couch later and later. And she seems very confused at times. Once I caught her just standing in the bathroom, holding a vase, clearly not sure how she or the vase got there.

Maybe she just needs proper nutrition. "Mom, do you want something to eat?"

Nothing. I swallow my irritation.

Sometimes I'll make her toast and eggs, or even

a complete meal like spaghetti. And there's all the freezer food. That's one good thing about a funeral. But it can be a bit like Russian roulette. You never really know what you'll find in there, especially when your dad is the vegetarian "butcher." People line up at his store, Slaughterhouse-Chive, every morning to buy vegetables that look *exactly* like meat, and so I guess a lot of people think everything they make for us *has* to be vegetarian.

I send my dad a text. I know he's working on a big order for a wedding—including one hundred vegan lamb-like chops. The hundreds of brief text bubbles on my screen are the only real evidence of our current relationship. **Minnie's corneas went to a guy who loves butterflies,** I text. **He wrote us.**

A minute later I get a reply. **I miss your sister's eyes.**

They were green.

He doesn't use her name. Ever.

I'm going to write back.

Maybe if my mom could hear how all the people who received Minnie's organs are doing, it would help her snap out of this fog. I want my mom's hugs back.

My dad replies with a turkey emoji. That probably means he's crafting a tofurkey.

I guess I will need to go through this organ-donation group. I'll start with my heart sister and try the direct approach first to see if this anonymity stuff is one-way. I sit down at the table and grab a sheet of paper.

Dear Heart Sister,

My name is Emmitt Highland, and I was happy to learn that you are the proud new owner of my twin sister's heart. Her name was Minnie. She was sixteen years old. She played the guitar but secretly preferred the ukulele, and she loved movies—maybe even as much as I do. You know, I'm having trouble separating out what of her was me, and what of me was her. You know? When you've spent every waking moment together, you sometimes wonder where one of you begins and the other ends. You wonder who you are.

Her friends were my friends. We spoke another language that no one understood. And no one ever will again.

But there was one thing my sister loved to do that we didn't share. Roadkill taxidermy. Yes, I'm totally serious. She made these incredibly detailed dioramas from trapped mice or squished squirrels she found on the walk home from school. She set them up like scenes in a movie, so they looked like humans playing video games or bungee jumping. Maybe you would like to come see them one day?

Please write us soon. Sorry for the slow reply. My mom's pretty sick—in story terms, you could call it her darkest hour. *She isn't thinking too clearly. Maybe I can come meet you?*

Sincerely,

Emmitt

I struggle with whether to sign it *Heart Brother*. I'm not sure I'm ready for that yet. Not with how everything around the organ donation went down.

I head to my bedroom to grab an envelope. On my desk is a diorama my sister created for me, one of her first. Not her best work. The suturing on the bodies is obvious, and there are signs she might not have cleaned the hides quite well enough, but it always makes me smile. A mouse shouts from a director's chair as other mice scurry about the set, one with a tiny mic boom, while two actor squirrels perform a fight scene. One squirrel is kicking the head of the other, who is falling forever to the ground. Minnie knew I want to be a film director.

In her more recent pieces, Minnie started combining different animals to create new creatures. Bird wings on chipmunks, mice heads on the body of a cat. Like a morbid Snow White, Minnie attracted dead animals. People brought her all kinds of deceased things— chipmunks, rabbits, a skunk once…even their own pets to be taxidermized. That's how my mom still has our dog to pat. Sirius died a year ago.

I stroke the nape of the director's fur, imagining him shouting orders. *Action! Cut!* I have this crazy idea. An idea that just might shove my mom off the couch. Might force my dad to whisper Minnie's name. Might fill this gaping hole in my chest.

TWO

It's not a crazy idea. It's brilliant.

If Minnie honored animals by making them whole again, then maybe I can piece my sister back together too. In a way. In *my* way. I just need to find out where all her organs went and then place them in a diorama—a living diorama of my creation.

I visualize the scene. My mom and dad listening to and laughing with all the pieces of Minnie, other people who each somehow have internalized her, making them more powerful, more artistic, more compassionate. They hug. We all hug, and it's like Minnie never left us.

Sunlight filters through the gauzy curtains of a bedroom now largely alien to me. The posters have been taken down, exposing chipped, burgundy-painted walls. Dusty pine shelves are nearly empty of books. The desk surface has been mostly decluttered except for broken pencils, a model of the flux capacitor from *Back to the Future* and the lonely diorama. Only a few items hang in the closet. My *Empire Strikes Back* duvet still covers my single bed, but I'm waiting for a new one. The stacked boxes around me are full of childhood stuff, things I want to leave behind, stuff that reminds me of Minnie more than it reminds me of myself. I'm sixteen now. Old enough to put away teddy bears, action figures and participation awards. The transformation started soon after Minnie's accident. The bare walls reflect my loss. But the boxes, whether full of me or of Minnie, I'm not sure I'm ready to give away just yet.

I push the boxes up against the walls and toss stray laundry items onto my bed, clearing a Minnie-sized space on the floor. I grab a roll of my dad's butcher paper from the closet and unroll it. I usually use it to brainstorm storyboards for movies, but today I need it to tell a different story. I always start with paper.

Laid out over the floor, waxen side down, the paper crinkles beneath my kneecaps. Three felt-tip markers—red, green and black—are on the nightstand. I have been using them to list the contents of the boxes. The acrid solvent smell of the uncapped black marker in my grip fills the room.

I draw Minnie's outline from memory. I haven't been able to look at a photo of her since the hospital. Even the picture of us cliff jumping together is face down on my shelf. But somehow her presence still fills my head as I begin. So often she would hang over my shoulder, bugging, suggesting, guiding.

The marker sweeps down, drawing her high forehead, a side-on profile of her face, cheeks, lips, everything plump, and a snub nose. My eyes fill with tears, but I keep drawing. I sit back to inspect the profile so far. It's not her.

It is a caricature of Minnie. Her ski-jump nose is too pointy, her lips bulbous. My stomach roils. I need to get this right. I flip the paper and face the blank page head-on—*like the accident?* I shudder and then press the palms of my hands against my temples to will the images away.

The marker nib squeaks as I continue, outlining her bobbed hair, the rounded shoulders that shook when she laughed. Arms out like she's ready for a hug. I'm hit with another wave of pain as I realize my sketch is starting to remind me of the chalk outlines in those old noir movie crime scenes. *Why is this so hard?* There's a quaver in the wrist I've drawn. A tear drips from the end of my nose and beads on the paper. It's not lost on me that I'm using butcher paper to map out the organs I need to collect. I'd be nauseated if I wasn't sure that Minnie would love it.

I sketch her hand. Gentle, firm, probing, never clammy—at least, not until they were...*fuh*...I keep drawing.

Her torso was solid. She always said she loved how strong her body was. She never worried about her size. I mean, as far as I know, and she's my best friend. *Knew. Was. Was my best friend.*

Our friendship made others jealous. We always knew what the other was thinking. We'd play games, telling people we could read each other's minds.

Then we'd prove it by guessing what the other was thinking. When our victims accused us of having planned it all in advance, we'd challenge them to give us categories—numbers, vegetables, animals, names. We'd always guess correctly, having played this game so often with each other. We shared what few friends we had—even her taxidermy group. But no one found their way into our inner circle of two. Still, though, sometimes I feel we all orbited her. I was just the moon, the closest thing in her sky.

When I start to draw her feet, I pause. If not flip-flops in summer or red patent-leather shoes at school, she wore bunny slippers. Actual former pet bunnies she named Left and Right the day she picked them from the Humane Society. They lived another two years before fulfilling their destinies. I could just do her barefoot—but her toenails were always a kaleidoscope of color, and the black marker can't do them justice. I sketch in long, droopy bunny ears.

Finally I have an outline of my sister on the floor. That single teardrop has sunk in, the splotch a sad earring. I weight the curling edges of the paper with four of her favorite books—*Calvin and Hobbes*, *Pet Sematary*, *Frankenstein* and a book of Walter Potter's curiosities.

I'm hit with another wave of pain. I sit back. The note from the guy who received her corneas crumples in my back pocket. I pull it out, smooth the envelope and shake the note free. It's short. Too short. My parents will need more than some letters and a map of Minnie's organs. But that's where I have skills. This past June

I spent more than half of my savings on a 360-degree video camera and virtual-reality gear. It's money I should be saving for after high school, but now there's only after Minnie.

I open my laptop and search *parts of the body*. It's odd how little I know about my own biology. Where is my liver? That thing I can't live without? Turns out it should be on the upper right of the abdomen. The kidneys on either side. The diaphragm—does that get transplanted? I know the stomach doesn't. The lungs do. Pancreas, intestines—ew. The heart. I begin to transfer their locations onto Minnie's outline.

My hand hurts from clenching the marker. The image of my sister's organs all piled together on the floor flashes in my brain. I draw deep breaths to clear the horrifying images.

I stop for a moment and use my phone to cue up the wireless speaker on my desk to put on my sister's favorite song, Jain's "Come." Not the score I would have picked for Minnie's movie, but I can hear the quirky fun in Jain's voice. I'd have chosen the theme from *8 Mile*, or maybe *Pulp Fiction*, but that would be me. I hit *play* and cue the entire *Guardians of the Galaxy* soundtrack to stream next.

I google *what parts of the body are used in organ donations*. Turns out a donor can save up to eight lives, but they can also improve the lives of over fifty people. I draw in some of the less likely parts carved from Minnie. *Harvested*. Skin, tendons, arteries, bone and eyes. Corneas.

When I finally meet the guy who has the corneas from Minnie's beautiful green eyes, I'll draw them on this outline as emerald butterflies. My heart sister may not have given me any clues, but he did.

The butterflies are how I will find him.

THREE

I'm guessing that the National Transplant Organization was founded long before social media existed.

It takes me fifteen minutes to figure out that people who hunt butterflies are called lepidopterists and that, in the Toronto area, only one posted on Twitter within days of my sister's organs being harvested.

I can see! he tweeted. His handle is @mothman62. I trace it to a YouTube user who, with a shaky phone video, has captured not only some unusual moth activity, but also two street signs that are only a twenty-minute bike ride from my house.

I stuff my camera, tripod and portable green screen into my backpack. The camera has multiple lenses and image-stitching technology that creates three-dimensional immersive views.

I've experimented with VR—virtual reality— all summer, and I often go to sleep with my headset on, watching my sister playing her uke or sewing a new arrangement. It's almost like she's still with me, only just beyond my reach. The scene I gravitate to most often is from a cottage weekend from a few months ago. My parents had splurged on a vacation. It was a treat. A family trip before we grew out of them, with Divina and Hal, a couple of our friends. After the parents had gone to bed, the four of us stayed up at the campfire, talking. Minnie asked me to get out my camera and film us. It was almost like she knew I would need it one day.

Once I was set up, Minnie started firing questions at us by the light of the fire. "What is your name?" "If you were an animal, what would you be?" "If I were to put you in a diorama, what would it look like?" Stuff like that. We were laughing and so not-serious. I'd thought it was just part of our vacation. But the answers. They surprised me.

Whenever panic rises within me, that rolling wave of paralyzing grief, I pull the headset over my eyes and join her at the fire. It's like I slide right under the wave.

I've decided that I'm going to ask her organ recipients those same questions. I'll bring them into our campfire and make Minnie whole.

A mere two hours after the delivery of a letter designed to keep us apart, I am on a street corner watching for Mothman. His social-media profile pic indicates I'm looking for a largish black guy in his late fifties. I am relieved to be out of the house. Even if it proves to be a dead end, stalking butterfly hunters is a hundred times better than staying inside all day listening to "For ten thousand dollars, who…"

I prop my bike against the street sign and settle in to wait. I check out passersby. Cars jerk over speed bumps. The flutter in my stomach feels appropriate. I honestly don't know what I'll learn from Mothman, but I know my parents need more than the writer's short thanks about seeing better. They deserve more than that. My sister does too.

A woman walks toward me along the sidewalk, tugging a little kid in a flouncing green dress. She has pigtails and ocean blue eyes. Will I recognize my sister in Mothman's eyes? Do I want to? The woman clears her throat, and I realize I've been staring at her child in what is probably a creepy way. I avert my gaze and try to shrink my six-foot-plus frame into something less threatening. They cross the street.

A dozen more people pass with curious looks as I scan each of them for signs of Mothman. Finally I spot a man squatting by a bush. It looks like he's holding a camera. From half a block away I can't discern his features, but he's wearing an inordinate amount of khaki, like he's on safari. I grab my pack and bike and slowly approach, the bike derailleur clicking. As I near, he cocks an ear, and I can tell he's no longer looking through the viewfinder of the camera, which is targeting something in the scraggly bushes.

He's huge. Gray spackles his cropped hair, and a constellation of freckles scatter across his face.

"Hi," I say. His gaze has such intensity that I can't help but hold it. "Mothman?" I whisper.

The eyes burn fiercer. Not the same color as Minnie's. His are brown.

"Who's asking?"

"You have my sister's corneas." A moment of stillness stretches as thought catches up to words. A car rips past, undercarriage crunching over a speed bump. He stands, eyes dancing over me in a quick appraisal, perhaps of my intent, maybe my potential to be dangerous, and then it's gone.

"You got my note."

"Off to catch butterflies," I say.

Mothman's lips split into a grin, and his arms envelop me, plunging my face into his shoulder, hands rubbing my spine, camera body digging into my chest. "It's all right, man. It's all right."

I force a laugh, trying to pull away from a kind of hug I haven't shared since the funeral, which even then had felt awkward and compulsory but somehow comforting too. "Thanks, thanks. I'm good, I'm fine." I pry free. Mothman's hand lingers on my shoulder. It feels heavy and too intimate. He drops his arm.

"I'm Emmitt. Emmitt Highland. Can I talk to you for a bit?" I ask.

"You kidding? Of course you can. I really want to talk to you too. My name's Gerry. Let's sit over there." He motions at a park bench and keeps talking as we walk toward it. "I'd hoped the note would work, but man, those transplanters really scour the letters. It was lucky my little clue managed to sneak through."

I struggle for words. It is so strange to be looking at this man, at his eyes, knowing a part of my sister is with him. I move my camera to my lap so the lens is between me and Mothman. This small barrier helps me to calm.

We sit silently for a minute. Mothman follows the flight path of a butterfly.

"The tweet helped," I say finally.

He looks like he is getting ready to hug me again. I scoot down the bench until I teeter on the edge. I lift my camera and zoom in on his face. If Minnie's here, I'll find her.

"Okay if I roll this thing? I'm working on a project," I say. I will have to hone my pitch for anyone else I track down.

"Sure, sure. I've been dreaming of meeting her, you know. Your sister. I wish there was some way I could thank her," he says. "I was a sniper in the army. Afghanistan. All sand and lost time. My eyes were everything. Until they weren't, and they discharged me. Honorably, sure, but not honorably here." He clutches his heart. "Know what I mean?" I shake my head. Talking to Mothman is like deciphering poetry. He sucks in a slow breath before continuing. "I can tell you all this. I can. We're family, right?" I swallow and nod. "Sure, we are. Well, I've never told anyone, but I once shot a man. A bad, bad man. From over a mile away. The sort of target that is so distant you need to factor in gravity. I counted four seconds before the guy dropped. I thought my eyes were everything."

I'm not sure what Minnie would think of having a

sniper receive her eyes, but I'm nodding from behind the frame of my shot, and I keep the camera rolling.

He lowers his gaze. "So whose eyes have I got?" he asks. "All they'd tell me was she was a young woman. All these years and I finally have a woman's perspective." His laugh fills the day. "How did your sister see the world?"

I swallow, at first not trusting speech. "Minnie was my twin sister. She was a total pacifist. Hated war." It's too much truth. "I'm sorry."

His eyes look back to his scuffed work boots, also khaki, and I realize it's his uniform. He's not on safari. He's on deployment. Or at least is dressing like he is.

"Yeah, I've had three lives—sniper, blind man, butterfly catcher. Guess which one I like the most?"

Mothman has a "before Minnie" and an "after Minnie" too. "I'm pretty sure she loved butterflies," I say in reply. "Live, still-fluttering ones."

"Well, I don't know many people, soldiers included, who don't hate killing things. But the butterflies...I only take pictures. I don't pin anything, man, just pictures." A tear tracks down his cheek.

"Sorry, Gerry, but my sister would totally pin a butterfly. Trust me." I burst out in a laugh that surprises me. "Minnie never had a good idea that didn't require needles."

"That's a fine thing then. I won't judge..." Gerry briefly covers his eyes with his fingers. "I'll take good care of these, son," he says.

I nod.

We sit in silence for a few moments, my camera still rolling. "How'd it happen?" he asks finally.

I shake my head. "She was hit by a car. The driver said she dashed into the road like she was trying to save something, but all there was on the road was a raven. She never regained consciousness."

"Saving the bird," he says.

"A long-dead bird," I reply.

Gerry clasps my forearm and elbow with his hands and says, "Well, Emmitt, if you ever need me, I'm here." He jerks his head toward an old house with a bowed porch roof and shingles that are starting to curl. "Just knock. If you want to hang out with me or just with her eyes."

It's not nothing, these words. I haven't seen Divina or Hal since the funeral. Maybe they're mourning too, and they don't have any space to offer. Or maybe they're uncomfortable around me, or they fear saying the wrong thing, or they think they're intruding. I try not to believe it's because they don't care. But part of me wonders, were they only Minnie's friends? Have they been boxed away with my room? I've never felt more alone. It's not nothing, Gerry's offer.

We stare at each other for a moment before his smile cracks again, and I start laughing. Briefly I really do have a piece of Minnie back. It gives me hope that maybe, if I manage to assemble the rest of her, the feeling will last forever.

"Gerry, I have a favor to ask," I say.

"I'd give you a kidney," he replies.

"Will you be in my movie?"

EXT. CAMPFIRE - NIGHT

Around the campfire, MINNIE
(16) sits with GERRY (late-50s).
She has her guitar across her
knees and plucks absently at
the strings without realizing
she's doing it. She grins at
him, face aglow, sparks flying
into the night.

> MINNIE
> What's your name?

> GERRY
> Gerry.

> MINNIE
> If you were an animal,
> what would you be?

> GERRY
> What? An animal?

"Run with it for a bit, okay?" I ask. Gerry shrugs and continues.

> GERRY
> I'd be a mongoose.

> MINNIE
> If I were to put you
> in a diorama, what
> would it look like?

> GERRY
> Diorama?

"Yeah, it's like a miniature slice of life," I say. "Anthropomorphic scenes. Imagine kids are running through an old-style museum and they see a mongoose you in your daily human life. What would it be doing?"

> GERRY
> This is bizarre.

"Well, that's my sister. During the winter she wore a coyote-head hat. A real one."

> GERRY
> Okay, well, my
> mongoose would be
> wearing a hat too.
> A top hat. Have one
> of those slick black
> canes. My coat, a big
> trench coat, would be
> on the ground for
> a lady mongoose to
> step on, and I'd be

tipping my hat in
appreciation, watching
all the other mon—
what's the plural?
Mongeese? Mongooses?
The others wandering
past. A gentleman. A
watcher. A mongoose.

                MINNIE
Cool. What would other
people put in your
diorama?

                GERRY
Jeez. How do they see
me, you mean?

Gerry's mouth tightens, and he
glances down at his hands, hands
that have pulled triggers.

                GERRY (CONT'D)
It'd be real different.
They'd put me on a
rooftop with a clear
line of sight for
my scope. Something
would be down there...
maybe a weasel.

26

> (beat)
> I've got a lot of
> brothers, sisters,
> moms and dads to
> answer to in the next
> life. I did my job—
> saved and protected
> many more people
> than I shot—but some
> people will only ever
> see a killer.

Gerry's shoulders slump,
defeated.

> MINNIE
> How can you make the
> diorama better?

> GERRY
> We're not really
> talking about
> dioramas anymore,
> are we?

"Were we ever?" I reply.

> GERRY
> Yeah, okay then, sure.
> I see where you're

going. You know how in
those dioramas
you can see the
glue coming unstuck
sometimes? Or where
some kid threw an
apple core into the
mouth of a T.rex in
an exhibit? I'm gonna
ignore that stuff. I
make my own diorama
better up here.

Gerry taps his head.

      GERRY (CONT'D)
When I see something
new, learn something
I never knew before,
that's a good day.
I don't think I can
fix the diorama—not
the one others see.
Just mine. There's a
reason why I chose
the mongoose as my
animal. They're immune
to snake venom. Eat
cobras for breakfast.

Gerry's jaw flexes, much as it
did on a mission, just before
he relaxed to take the shot.

        GERRY (CONT'D)
    I will refuse to see
    hate. Ever see a
    pipevine swallowtail
    caterpillar? Ugliest
    damn things.
    But such beautiful
    butterflies.
        (beat)
    I will look for the
    beautiful in every
    ugly thing.

Gerry's eyes shine with
determination. Minnie grins.

        FADE OUT.

I think Minnie's eyes are in the right place.

After I finish filming, Gerry looks at me. "You going to show me what you're doing with all that?"

"At the end," I say. "When this is over."

FOUR

The phone rings. And rings. I'm holding my mom's bra. No one else has done the laundry for weeks. Having washed the clothes on *delicate*, I'm now hanging them to dry on a line that spans the basement ceiling. My dad used to do the laundry. I started doing my own when I ran out of clean clothes to wear. Then I began washing my parents' after theirs began to reek. Already the line sags with my dad's underwear. I pick up a green sock—my sister's—from the basket. It must have been left in the dryer from an old load. I move to toss it into the garbage, stop myself, ball it up and throw it behind the dryer. I pick up another mom-bra. The phone keeps ringing. I drop the bra back into the laundry basket, wipe my hands on my shirt and run up the stairs to grab the kitchen handset.

It's a woman named Martha from the National Transplant Organization.

"We're looking for Emmitt Highland."

"Here," I say, breathing hard.

"Hello, Mr. Highland. We received your letter but regret that we are unable to forward it on to the organ recipient. It contains too much personal information. It's important that the recipient not have any way to contact you."

"I was hoping maybe the donor family could make contact if they wanted to."

"Sorry, no, the process is entirely anonymous."

I frown into the phone. "Even if we both agree that we want to talk?"

"Under no circumstances will we connect you."

"Why?"

"There are reasons for anonymity."

"None that make any sense."

Through the kitchen doorway I see my mom prop herself up on her elbows and scowl at me. I have finally found something that makes her listen.

"Sorry," I say into the phone, extra loud for my mom. "I guess I understand the whole medical privacy thing." But I really don't.

"You're welcome to send a new letter, but please keep the details generic."

I sigh. The whole reason I wasn't satisfied with my heart sister's letter was because it had been so generic. I'll try again. Or I'll try to find another way to contact her.

I hang up. My mom slumps back on the couch. The TV is off, but she still stares at the blank screen.

"Do you want a snack?" I ask her. "When is Dad getting back?"

But she ignores me like the ringing phone. I flip the TV on, disturbed by the lack of distraction.

I get that Minnie was their favorite. She was my favorite person too.

My parents hadn't said anything when I started clearing the walls and shelves of my room. Movie posters of *Chinatown*, *Brazil*, *Citizen Kane*. A papier mâché horse head, modelled after the iconic one from *The Godfather*. (Minnie had promised to make me an even more realistic one as soon as she found the right "supplies.") Christmas lights I'd strung on the wall to copy the setup from *Stranger Things* with *SLEEP* spelled out instead of *RUN*—Minnie's idea. Maybe my parents understood. All of us pulled the plug on my life at home, just as they had done on Minnie six weeks earlier.

I'll set the scene.

After the accident, Minnie hadn't drawn a breath on her own for two days, but that didn't mean she was dead.

The doctors weren't hopeful. Minnie had *severe traumatic brain injury* from when her head struck the pavement. The ER staff had worked for two hours to resuscitate her before getting a stable heartbeat, but they'd told us later that Minnie's prognosis was poor. I hadn't given up. I had snuck close to the room where they treated her. Through the window I could see Minnie was a web of tubing. "Head injuries make for good organs," I heard one doctor say. I swear he rubbed his hands together. Fingers long and delicate like those of a pianist. Perfect for the tender motor skills of excising and suturing.

This had been a dark hour.

Two days later, in the pediatric intensive care unit, signs of the accident were already sliding away. Bruises had gone from red to purple to yellow. On the ventilator, Minnie was healing. Not dead. Her skin was pink and warm.

I had yet to leave the hospital. If she was there, I was staying.

I watched the first test for brain death. We were all encouraged to. Said it might help. I had gone into a rage at the mention of Minnie's wishes for organ donation. "But she's not dead!" I had cried.

New staff—not part of Minnie's PICU team, not Dr. Lebow, but a doctor who said he was a respiratory therapist and a new nurse—explained that they would now test for a permanent loss of all integrated brain function.

The respiratory therapist, a man with the hint of an Eastern European accent who looked like he tossed medicine balls around in his free time, knuckled my sister's sternum with meaty fingers.

I glanced at my parents, expecting them to object, but they looked on, eyes wide and expectant, watching for a miracle. With the machines' alarms off, silence hung thick. I turned back to the two strangers poking at my sister.

"We are looking for any form of response," he said. "Increases in heart rate, vocalization, a grimace." He leaned across Minnie, and I imagined her cringing from his breath. With his thumbs on her brow ridge and his fingers gripped around her head, his knuckles whitened as he pressed, arms trembling with force. I reached up and pushed a thumb into my eyebrow, feeling the pain. I gritted my jaw. Minnie didn't budge, but the marks from the thumbs remained red and angry against her brow.

"You're hurting her," I said.

"She can't feel it," the nurse said.

"We're making sure she can't feel it," the doctor with the meaty hands clarified.

He shifted to her hand, pinched one nail bed and then another, watching her face and then breathing noisily through his nostrils.

"I'll do cranial nerve tests next," he explained, bringing out a slim light and prying open Minnie's eyelids, first one and then the other, the light flashing in and then away. Always her pupils remained wide. That was what they were looking for. I'd seen enough cop shows to know. They were looking for her pupils, the black holes in the center of her eyes, to constrict with the light. Minnie's endlessly gaped.

My mom reached for Minnie. Her fingers twitched at the touch.

I leaped up, pointing and gawking.

"There," I cried, joy so ready to push past the fear in my chest. "Her hand. It moved."

My mom snatched hers away, crying out.

The doctor shook his head no. "Spinal reflexes," he said. "It's not a sign of life. I'm sorry—I should have explained that you will see these. Minnie's spine has nerves, and what you're seeing is a signal traveling from the hand to the spine and then back to the hand."

"But never to the brain stem," the second doctor added.

The nurse poured water from a pitcher filled with ice into a measuring cup. More tests. Hope remained.

"Some of our cranial nerves have direct connections, and we can try to stimulate them. The optical nerve with the light. The vestibular nerves with cold-water irrigation." The doctor pointed to the nurse. "I'm looking for eye movement." With a nod, the nurse trickled the icy water into Minnie's ear. We all watched Minnie's eyes. They didn't move.

"That's it then," my dad whispered.

"There is one more test. It's called the apnea test," the doctor explained. "We withdraw ventilator support and look for signs of respiration."

The nurse dabbed at Minnie's ear with a cloth while the second doctor wiggled the breathing tube. That was when the respiratory therapist turned down the ventilator, and I watched as Minnie's breathing slowed, then stopped. It happened so quickly, I didn't have time to prepare.

Choked silence. A checked watch.

No breath.

Breathe, I urged.

Still Minnie remained pink and warm.

Breathe!

The heart monitor flashed and then flatlined. "You're killing her!" I screamed. "You're killing—"

But I didn't have a chance to say more. Dr. Lebow was in the room, pulling me out and herding my malleable, agreeable parents.

"The oxygen level dropped too low," Dr. Lebow said. "It happens. We'll complete the whole test again," she replied, as if that would appease me.

"You touch her, and I'll shove a breathing tube down your throat."

She blanched, swallowed and then said to my parents, "It might be best for Emmitt to sit the next test out."

I wasn't invited for the final round. I was relegated to the waiting room.

While I waited I wondered if any of the other families were already here, waiting for Minnie's organs. It was good I wasn't in her room. The next doctor I caught knuckling my sister's sternum would have my knuckles cracking against their jaw.

I slumped in a light blue plastic molded chair, one of a row bolted to the floor. They were surprisingly comfortable—until you lay across the row of them to sleep. Then the curves in the plastic dug into your hip, calf and neck.

My mom was in watching the tests. My dad was out for a walk. Which meant he was smoking, a vice he had given up the day we were born—I guess it had really been for Minnie.

Every year when my mom had cut up the wallet-sized school pictures, I'd tucked the photo of my sister into that back fold where I stored assorted loyalty cards for coffee shops and movie theaters, a climbing-gym membership and long-expired coupons. I pulled the collected photos out. Was this why my mother had given them to me? Just in case I needed to remember my sister? I had four. Four years had elapsed since I'd bought this wallet from a vendor on Queen Street. I regretted the other photos I had tossed, frayed and faded, along with the old wallet and its collection of illegible receipts—receipts that had been important enough to carry around for years.

It used to be that there might be an organ donation card with the receipts. Now you needed to register online. I hadn't—hadn't realized I could at sixteen—but Minnie had. Minnie who wasted nothing, not even a skunk much loved by car tires. Minnie had registered not two weeks before the accident, on our birthday. My parents had hesitated in their decision until they'd been informed of her registration by the liaison. *It is what she wanted. Wants.*

The double doors leading to the ward swung open, and my mom stepped through. When she caught sight of me in my usual chair she stopped, her shoulders slumped, and she sobbed. Minnie had failed the test. She had never failed a test in her life.

She was dead. Clinically so. Brain dead.

On a scrap of paper, I sketched out a planned tattoo.

Minnie's heart was still beating. *Not dead, not dead, not dead.*

In my bedroom I kneel beside the outline I've drawn of Minnie and pick up the green marker. I drop it, open the box of markers and grab a brown instead. I draw big brown-colored moths over her eyes.

On my shoulder the tattoo still aches, even now. A large Do Not Recycle sign in green and red. I had to lie about my age to get the tattoo. I'm old enough to donate a kidney, but not to put a bit of ink on my skin.

I lie down and place my hand on Minnie's paper one.

"I'll find you," I promise her and the ceiling's glow-in-the-dark stars.

I want to find more Mothmans. Eight Mothmans equal one Minnie. I turn on my side and place my palm over her missing heart. I will find my heart sister.

I push myself upright, draw a deep breath and pull my laptop from a canvas backpack. I begin to search different social-media platforms for news of happy parents, brothers, sisters, uncles and aunts— anyone who might have a piece of Minnie. I scan back as far as the day of Minnie's death. The day the doctors harvested her organs. Keywords: *new heart*, *heart transplant*, *gift of life heart*, *heart donation*. The organ registry is national, but, given the millions of people who live in Toronto, there's still a good chance Minnie's organs went to nearby recipients. I scour the internet first for my heart sister and then review her letter—for the hundredth time—in search of identifying information.

It's surprising how few mentions on social media there are from organ recipients. Is it because they know this joy has come at someone else's expense? Do they fear that their joy dishonors the loss of others?

It doesn't. I know. As my mom pats another tuft from glassy-eyed Sirius, she knows. As my dad painstakingly colors tofu to look like barbecued chicken skin, he knows. The recipient's joy could lessen our grief though, right? The sum of the joy might replace the loss of the whole. Mom's an accountant, so I know about balance sheets and income statements. Assets and liabilities. Profits and losses. If we add all the joy, we *will* cut our losses.

I spot a tweet about a brother who received a new heart in Tampa, Florida. One about a mother who died on the wait list. Another transplant recipient in Canada, a girl who received a liver, but the donor was the living father. That made the press. They could talk about it.

I try other organs—kidneys, pancreas, all of them—until finally I find a public Facebook post from a woman who received new lungs. She lives in Peterborough, a couple of hours from Toronto. Close enough that I can take the bus if I can figure out where she lives.

I post on all the platforms I can think of.

Seeking: Recipients of my sister's organs. If you or someone you know received an organ on July 1, please contact me. I sound so crazy. Please share. I only want to know that my sister helped others.

I notice Mothman has tagged me on an Instagram post. It's a photo of a tiny gray moth on a large pink flower—a peony, I think. The flower stem is bent by the weight of the flower, but the way he's captured the moth on the verge of taking off makes it look like it's holding the flower up. #goodday is the hashtag.

I smile and message the lungs lady, asking if I can meet her. I get the familiar sense of butterflies in my stomach, and I start to think perhaps it's my sister telling me I'm doing the right thing.

Nothing can stop me now.

FIVE

With the VR headset tight over my eyes, I look across the campfire at Minnie and then twist to Gerry. They're both frozen. He's mid-laugh, face bright. She is leaning forward, legs folded like a yogi. I've been up for a few hours, testing the footage. The software has neatly spliced Gerry from the greenscreen video shot on the park bench and placed him on one of the six logs that surround the fire. My point of view is just in front of the fire itself, so that if I try to look down at my feet, they're nearly in the flames. I press *play* on the hand controller, and Minnie says, *"If I were to—"*

At a bleep on my phone, I pause the playback and push up the headset.

A reply to my post: Hi, my brother got a new liver around then. Maybe it was your sister's? I need you to talk to him.

I set the headset down on the desk and message her. Thanks! Can you give me his info, and I'll set it up?

The response is quick. **He doesn't want to meet you.**

With my thumbs poised over the phone's keyboard, I frown. ???

I'm not sure how else to respond.

The person adds, **Would you mind showing up though? You'll understand when you meet him.**

Perhaps if I had more to lose I would argue, but I don't. This meeting with the liver guy might be weird, but it's another hit, someone to add to the cast list while I work toward tracing the star of the show.

Where are you, and when do you want me?

We're in Hamilton. I'll send the address. The earlier the better.

Their profile pic shows a young woman captured in mid-jump on a beach. Any other details are hidden. She flips me the address.

I smile at the actor squirrels and turn to the Minnie sketch on the floor. Her liver looks like a giant lima bean.

I hit the washroom, then the kitchen. I peek into the living room. Sirius's eyes sparkle at me from near the couch, tail stuck mid-wag, rubber tongue lolling. "Hey, boy, thanks for taking care of Mom." She won't be up for hours.

I hear Dad's footsteps thudding down the hall. His beard precedes him. Shot with gray, it matches his eyes. He stumbles to the coffee pot, sloshes yesterday's coffee around, then seems to think better of drinking it.

"I'll brew you some fresh," I say.

He shakes his head. "Have to go."

"Dad—"

"Emmitt, I have twenty cauliflowers to carve into sheep."

He used to laugh when he said stuff like this, but now he seems stressed about it.

"You could call it a cauliflock," I suggest.

His lips give the barest twitch as he grabs his keys and heads out.

I grind some beans and leave the fresh pot to percolate for Mom. After I eat a piece of toast, I write a note saying that I'm off to film a movie. She won't read it, but it makes me feel better. On my way out I spot that familiar envelope in the mailbox, and I rip it open:

Dear Heart Family,

Your letter has probably been caught by the Gatekeepers of Nodo (sounds like a book title, huh?). Let me try to answer some possible questions. I am young. Although I have had a sick body, I am grateful for having had a decent mind. If I were to have a superpower, it would be to speed-read. The quality I most value is trust. I think it's because so much of my life is out of my control. Trusting hasn't failed me yet. But I also envy people who have courage. I think envy tells us a lot about who we are and what is important to us. I envy the brave. In some ways, I'm still searching for a heart.

Your Heart Sister, Heart Daughter

Trust. The only person I've ever trusted completely was Minnie. No matter if we were separated by distance or time, I knew she'd have my back. And she was oh so brave. But she's left me. And now I'm also searching for a heart.

"Hi, Emm." I glance up from the note and quickly fold it away. Divina and Hal stand at the base of the steps. Hal is holding a bag with a dead squirrel, quite possibly the one I saw yesterday flattened on the street. Divina clutches a wooden box with one hand and twists a braid with the other.

"Sorry for not calling," she says. "We have something for your family."

Six weeks have passed since I last saw these two roadkill scavengers. Before my sister died, we regularly hung out in Minnie's garage workshop, me helping with the arrangements of their taxidermic scenes—the stories— them stitching and scraping. I'd thought we were friends. But *it's been six weeks*.

"You've been working on stuff, I guess," I say.

"Yeah, we went back to the scene of…you know…" Hal says, holding up the squirrel but looking at the house eaves.

"Sure."

Divina lifts the box for me to take.

I flip the brass hasp and open the lid.

In the dull light, the raven's feathers are oily and dark. A clock is set in its chest. I cringe from it. They've mounted the raven Minnie died trying to scavenge.

Hal says, "We guessed at when to set the time."

The clock is brass with a white face and black hands.

"We thought your mom and dad would—"

"What the hell, guys?" I ask. "My mom can't get off the couch. My dad can't even say Minnie's name. And you think they want to see a dead raven with a clock stuck in it?"

"We just—"

"No, we don't need any more reminders that she's dead. No more dead stuff. None!"

Divina grits her teeth, jaw flexing. "Minnie would have loved it."

"I...am...not...Minnie!"

I slam the door on them and then realize I'm still holding the raven in its box. The lid snaps shut. Before my mom can ask what it is, I take it to the basement and shove it behind the Halloween decorations.

It takes about an hour to get to Hamilton by train, a real milk run with a dozen station stops and brief flashes of a silver lake between. I haul all my gear down the streets, heading toward the steel mills. Sweat courses down my back and neck. When I'm ten minutes out, I warn the sister that I'm close. She says she'll meet me in front of the house. By the time I'm almost there, my sweatshirt itches and my jeans have rubbed my thighs raw.

Liver Brother lives on a street of single-family bungalows with well-tended red, pink and white rosebushes. My home feels far away, as if I've traveled overseas. Older men and women lounge on or sweep out porches that sport Italian and Canadian flags.

Their brooms kick up puffs of white dust. Many eyes watch as I stop and lower my messenger bag to the sidewalk. The scratching brooms pause.

I consider leaving. If Liver Brother doesn't want to see me, why would I want to see him? Stares burn into my back. Smoke scratches at my throat, reminding me of my father. Would he be smoking again if it had been me hit by that car?

The cool shade of the porch beckons. Inside could be another Mothman. Someone else searching for connection.

Suddenly the front door opens. A small middle-aged woman stands there.

"Emmitt?" she asks wearily. She glances at the neighbors on their porches and gives them a nothing-to-see-here smile. They watch. A man takes a slow sip of coffee. A broom resumes sweeping.

She shoulders my bag as if it's nothing and hustles me indoors. "My brother's in the back. He'd love to hear about your sister."

In the living room off the hall, I can see two young boys playing video games. They don't look up from the couch. The woman disappears into the kitchen. I smell tomatoes and garlic.

"In the back?" I ask.

"In the back," she says. Something clangs. Water runs.

I slide off my shoes and try to ignore my thirst. "What's his name?" She sticks her head out of the hole and cups her hand to her ear. "My liver brother," I say. "What's his name?"

She swallows. "His name is Joey. I'm Carina."

Beyond the kitchen are three doors—two are open. One room is a washroom full of gray marble and the other, I assume, is Joey's room. Even before I knock, the smell of stale sweat and alcohol overwhelms the pasta sauce.

I'm starting to put everything together. Why Joey's sister wanted me to come. Why someone often needs a new liver in the first place. What I'm here for.

It's a setup.

Anger lances through me as I rap my knuckles against the door frame. "Joey?"

A groan and then a muffled thump as something hits the floor. The sounds of cooking have stopped, leaving only the muted discharging of video-game lasers. Light struggles through curtains, producing a weak glow that doesn't reach the bed where some moldering, fetid lump hunkers beneath a black silk duvet.

Why is it that I feel uncomfortable walking up a neighbor's path to knock on their door, yet here I am at the threshold to some stranger's room and I feel entitled to be here?

"Joey," I say, and I switch on the light.

Joey sits up, head coming forward on his neck as he peers blearily at me. "Who the hell are you?"

Now I know why the transplanters don't want us meeting each other.

"I'm your liver brother, you jerk. And you're killing my sister."

SIX

Rage holds my tongue as my eyes adjust to the low light.

Stringy hair hangs over Joey's eyes. The earlier thump was from a bottle that fell off the bed and rolled out onto the carpet.

I begin quietly. "My name is Emmitt. You received my sister's liver. Minnie was sixteen years old, in perfect health, and the most amazing person in my world. You've been given her liver and you're wasting it? No, *first-degree murdering* it!"

My final shout rings out, and the sounds of video games disappear.

"Yeah." Joey shakes his head and slumps back. "I don't deserve it. You're right. So what're you going to do about it?"

I glance back. In the hall Carina stares. Each of her arms holds one of the boys tight to her hip. Her expression fuels more frustration—she's using me—and the weight of unwanted responsibility.

"How'd he even get a liver?" I ask her. The kids run back to the living room. "Aren't there rules?"

"Joey was sober. Six months sober. But addiction's a disease," Carina says. "I've watched him try. It's hard."

"So when he was about to die he could stop drinking long enough to qualify for an organ, but not now that he's hit the Reset button?"

Carina has no answer, only imploring eyes. My hands tremble, and I head back toward the front door.

"Please," she says as I pass. "Please!"

I stop next to the washroom. I'm parched, and the thought of climbing to the train station again without water overpowers my desire to flee.

"Yes, yes." Carina waves me inside.

I run cool water over my hands and then my face. My heart rate slows. I am able to think again. What would Minnie say? What would she do? Rage is what Joey is looking for. He wants people to give up on him so that the shame of drinking won't hurt as much. There was a big cross on his wall. I step out of the bathroom and return to Joey's room. Carina follows me.

"Are you in Alcoholics Anonymous, Joey?" I ask.

"Tried AA," Carina answers.

"Did you have a sponsor?"

"He hasn't gone since—"

"Well, you have a new sponsor." I'm letting Minnie do the talking. "Yeah, she's one you can't avoid because she's inside of you. Here's the deal. Do you *want* to stop drinking?"

There's a protracted pause. But then Joey finally speaks.

"Yes. Not for me. For them."

Joey looks down the hall at the two boys on the couch. That's when I realize he's not their uncle but their father.

"Okay, then. Let's get going."

Slowly Joey nods.

"Climb out of bed."

I don't know how to treat alcoholism. All I know is my sister is here with us. I sense her fingers on my shoulder, light as a butterfly, guiding me. Joey swings his legs over and plants his feet on the plush carpet.

He shuffles toward me and stops before he reaches the door. His breath billows rank and sour.

"You can drink, Joey," I say. "You can drink as much as you want." He glances at me with a tiny furrow in his brow. "No one can stop you. But on behalf of my sister, I'm going to call you every day. *Every* day. And I'll ask you three questions." I think fast.

"Why do you want to live? Why were you worth saving? And how will a drink help you? That's the deal, understand?"

Joey doesn't look like he understands, but he nods.

But I'm not done yet. I grab the bottle of vodka from the floor and shake it, the small amount left sloshing. "Drink!"

Joey's hands clench.

"No? Why not?" I ask. "Why do you want to live?" This is no longer Minnie guiding me. This is full-on, raging Emmitt.

His shoulders give a hitch, and his cheeks blow out in a suppressed sob. He stares past me down the hall.

"You want to live for your boys," I say. "Okay, so why are you worth saving? Why you over some other guy who's been sober for years or who didn't trash his own liver? He might have kids too."

"Hey, that's enough!" Carina's shout echoes.

I can tell by the pain in Carina's face that she thinks I've pushed too far, that she's having second thoughts about having brought me here, but I don't care. I hadn't realized Minnie still requires saving, even if it is only a piece of her. We're gonna bond, Joey and me.

Finally Joey shakes his head. "I don't know," he whispers.

As my rage subsides again, I remember my film. Minnie at the campfire. Minnie asking her questions. "Joey, you don't have to answer to me," I say. "But you do have to answer to her."

His expression twists, and his face flushes. "I don't have to—"

"I'm working on a project, something I hope will provide comfort for a lot of people, including you. Will you help me?"

His eyes flash down the hall again. He nods.

"Thank you," I say. "I'm going to set up my equipment, and then I want you to answer some questions."

He nods and pushes past us. Carina stares at me. Her gaze travels to my hands, which are shaking, but not from rage anymore. Excitement. This is my job now. Making sure Minnie lives on.

I unzip my backpack and begin setting up my camera rig. I dig out the VR headset.

A few minutes later Joey returns. He has run a brush through his hair and splashed water on his face.

"Joey," I say. "Meet my sister, Minnie."

He stiffens as I slip the headset over his scalp.

```
EXT. CAMPFIRE - NIGHT

Around the campfire, MINNIE
(16) sits with JOEY (mid-30s).
She has her guitar across her
knees and plucks absently at
the strings without realizing
she's doing it. She grins at
him, face aglow, sparks flying
into the night.

                MINNIE
        What's your name?
```

I pause the playback after each question, so he can remove the headset and answer to the camera. He's pale against the green sheet and subdued, now having met Minnie. "Yeah, that's her," I say.

```
                JOEY
        Joey.
```

> MINNIE
> If you were an animal,
> what would you be?

After Gerry, I half expect Joey to stumble here, but he seems to buy into this line of questioning, answering quickly.

> JOEY
> A ferret.
> > (beat)
> Yeah. They're like
> little weasels.
> Thieves.

> MINNIE
> If I were to put you
> in a diorama, what
> would it look like?

With the headset off, Joey's eyes dart toward the bottles of liquor.

> JOEY
> Easy. Face down in
> the dirt. Tiny bottles
> all around. Maybe
> those airplane-sized
> bottles. One still in
> my hand.

Two little ferrets
staring on.
    (swallows)
When I wake up, I
think about my first
drink. How I will get
it. How I can find my
second. Where to hide
the empties. It's my
world. I tell myself
that I can stop
tomorrow. But, even
drunk, I already know
I'm lying.

Joey fidgets with his hands.
There's more he wants to say.

    JOEY (CONT'D)
But it wasn't like
that...not always. My
Leah. My Leah. She
was my wife. I'm a
widower. She'd be a
lynx. So much stronger
than me. She should
have lived. She danced
with the boys. She
sang. She worked
so hard. Ferret me

would just have been
watching her.

MINNIE
Cool. What would other
people put in your
diorama?

JOEY
There would be
more ferrets. Other
animals. Mice,
rabbits—they'd be
protecting me even
though I'd eat them if
I could stand.

Joey looks up, surprised.

JOEY (CONT'D)
They're lifting me.
One might be putting
another bottle in my
hand. She knows my
brand of vodka. I'm
grieving still. They
think I drink because
I'm sad. It makes
it okay. They'd be
hugging me. Carina,

you're there too...

        MINNIE
How can you make the
diorama better?

        JOEY
I need to dump the
bottles, right? I need
to push myself up onto
my knees. Brush myself
off. Stand. Show the
two little ferrets I
can be strong myself.
That they don't need
drugs.

Joey's eyes search for
something far, far away.
Minnie grins back. There's
doubt in the slump of Joey's
shoulders. This isn't his
first intervention. These are
steps.

            FADE OUT.

"And cut," I say.

After Joey finishes, he stares at me. "She didn't ask
why I should live."

"You answered that question," I say.

With a final glance at Carina and the boys, he tears the edge from a sheet of paper. "We can try." He writes on the scrap and hands it to me. "My phone number. Call around four. That's when it's toughest."

Tears flow freely down Carina's face. "I'm sorry, Joey. I'm still here though. Still here."

My anger at her using me is spent. I realize now that Minnie's gift isn't only for the recipient. Maybe it isn't fair that this guy collected my sister's liver, and maybe it is. But every recipient has a family too. Joey's sister and his boys needed Minnie's liver as much as he did. That's what's keeping him alive.

SEVEN

On the train back home, I write a note to my heart sister. In it I add a series of spelling errors and omissions. If she catches the code, I hope she'll contact me.

Dear Heart Sistr,

What's it like to have sommeone else's heart? An I right to feel that you owe my sester somehing? I don' mean that in a bad way, only that sould the donor or the donor famely have any rihts? I met someone today tat wasn't treating their gift very well.

Enough about that though. I want to telll you about my sister, but I can't. I caann only tell you that your heart is loving and caring and so so strong. How are you doing? Heart surgery can't have been easy!?

<3<3<3<3d
Heart Bro

So it's a bit obvious, but I imagine the censors as little old men and women who think teenagers can't spell without software correcting them.

The sizzling of quasi-bacon and a salty soy smell greets me as I arrive. Dad must have brought home some of his work for dinner. Before Minnie died, this would have been only marginally tastier than pulling something random from the freezer, but definitely more entertaining. I've been doing most of the cooking lately, though, and it bothers me now that he didn't check with me first.

Seasoned ground soy is really the closest he can come to real meat, and he has turned that into sorta-burgers, not-meatballs, meatless tacos and somewhat-sausage. But he's most creative when someone asks him to make food for vegetarians that looks like what everyone else is having. Like they're worried the vegetarians at the wedding will feel left out when everyone else is having roast beef.

"I was planning on pizzas."

"But I'm home," my dad replies.

"I would have skipped the cheese on your pizza."

On a plate in the kitchen are bits and pieces from a number of customer orders—crab, steak and lamb chops. He adds bacon, sliding it off the pan. All are made from processed vegetables, carefully textured and dyed. Beside the bacon he spoons a side of peas. How weird is it that vegetables pretending to be meat need to be balanced with real vegetables?

I pull back my anger, wondering if it followed me from Joey's. I'm tired.

"The lamb isn't vegan," my dad says. "I had to use some egg as a binder."

"Makes sense," I reply.

"As much as anything does."

"Mom," I call, "you coming to eat?" There's no plate set for her.

On the television, the game-show host asks, "What percentage of the world lives in poverty?"

Mom doesn't answer me or the television. But she does start sobbing.

I go to her and shift Sirius down so that I can sit beside her.

Tears pour down her cheeks. "I don't even know why I'm crying," she says. "It's all so pointless. You know?" She sobs again. "People are starving, and everyone's rushing around with cell phones in cars, hitting people so they can hit *send* on a text..." My mom suspects the car that hit my sister was traveling too fast, the driver distracted by his phone. But the driver says otherwise, that Minnie was the distracted one. I imagine her fearful that the raven's feathers, iridescent in the dying light, would be traumatized by car tires.

"I know, I know." I lean down and wrap one arm around her rigid shoulders. "It'll get better, Mom."

She spasms, clenching her stomach, hands balled into fists. "It hurts so much. I wish...I wish I'd never had her."

I strangle the cry that erupts from my throat.

"Really, Emmitt, the pain of loss is greater than the misery of love. Isn't it?" She wants a real answer to that.

Something that isn't hopeless. "How can I cook when everything I make she used to eat? How can I shop when she used to sit in those same shopping carts? How can I turn on music when all I hear is your sister strumming her guitar? Everything is gone."

"I'm working on something, Mom. I'll prove to you it's not all gone." I want to show them that Minnie's legacy is so much greater than they think. But I need to do better than Joey.

She sniffles and shuts her eyes. "I don't know how you do it," she says. "Do you even feel?"

I hold her quavering gaze. Unable to speak. *Do I feel?* Sometimes I feel like a sailboat in a roiling but windless ocean. Everything I do, I do so I won't need to feel so much. I won't be like my mom. Useless. Abandoning.

"How can you not see?" I ask. Maybe if I wasn't doing the cooking, the laundry, the carrying on, I'd have enough will to show my heartbreak.

I kiss her on the forehead. Her clawed hands shake. For the first time, I wonder how much time I have before my mother loses herself entirely.

My dad has taken his plate and left the kitchen. A wave of loneliness folds over me, causing me to sway. Is there any difference between my mom, who, in the weight of her depression, has left an imprint of herself on the couch, and my father, who is almost as ghostly a presence in the house as my sister? I stagger, listing one way and then the next, to my plate. Beside it is another letter. I grasp it and hold on.

Dearest Heart Family,

Wow, these one-way letters are tricky. You're like a crappy boyfriend. Give me something here!

It's hard to talk about the past without giving you too much information about myself, so let's talk about the future, all right?

I want to travel. When you have a bad heart, travel is tough. There are medications that need to be kept up and blood levels that need to be measured. I was on thinners— not anymore!—and health insurance is expensive, even if you can qualify. So, travel. Did your daughter have a heart's desire? A place she desperately wanted to go? Maybe a place where she was at peace? If so, I'll go there. I promise.

What sort of music do you like? I figure if I can listen to the same music you are, we'll be connected by it.

At nine o'clock for the next couple of nights, listen to "Nothing Else Matters." I will too. And I'll be there. Bonus points if you have a copy of Dune somewhere. I'll be reading from the beginning. But I read fast.

I love you,
Heart Daughter/Sis

Dune. I shake my head at that. We can do so much better than *Dune*. How about *The Godfather*, *American Psycho*, *No Country for Old Men*, *Fight Club*? I'd even take *Pride and Prejudice*. Maybe it's because these are all books that were made into movies, but so was *Dune*— just a bad movie.

Although the letter is addressed to my family, I feel as though she is speaking to me. Clearly she hasn't received my latest letter and doesn't realize we can move past this crazy shuttling of letters between us and the organization. Maybe they caught the code?

I'm smiling as I jog into my room, thinking about those books and how good stories are like good friends. I peel the packing tape off a box and start pulling out paperbacks. My tattered copy of *Dune* smells of dust, and its pages are as fragile as butterfly wings. I spot *The Godfather* in the stack and wonder why I was so quick to pack it away. I search out other favorites, sigh at the comfortable weight of *The Count of Monte Cristo* and then slot them back onto the bookshelf and close the box.

I leave *Dune* next to my bed, the letter tucked inside, before searching out the song she mentioned. I've never heard it before, but I recognize the heavy metal band that sings it and cue up Metallica's entire album on my phone. My letter to my heart sister seems so uninspired now by comparison to hers, so I write her another one, one that tells her how I didn't know Metallica well, but if we're talking nineties music, she should check out the soundtrack to the movie *Trainspotting* or the indie horror flick *The Faculty*. And that we should definitely listen to my sister's favorite song together at least once and read *Pet Sematary*—even though I've only ever seen the movie— and how Minnie related to Calvin in *Calvin and Hobbes*.

Writing about Minnie relaxes me. I feel my heart sister close. I wish my parents could have this. It would make it easier for them. It will.

I close the letter with the words *I love you too.* And I can't really explain the instalove in my gut, except that she has my sister's heart and my sister always had mine.

EIGHT

My sister created a diorama she called *Rat Race: Mouse Wins*. She always said that I inspired it, that when we were little she had watched from the sidelines of our grade-school track meet. It was the 1,500-meter race, and I had been this dumpy, short kid. I don't remember a thing, but it left an impression on her, and the diorama immortalizes it.

In the scene are eight runners. Minnie used what she could for participants, and since this was during an unfortunate infestation of rats—those I remember entering at our sewer pipe, chewing through concrete— this diorama has seven rats and a mouse. You can guess who the mouse is supposed to represent. Anyway, all these rats are running flat out, tails straight back, while the mouse is standing up on its hind legs, skipping and looking around with this grin on its face, as if it's not in a race at all but at a county fair, checking out the rides and cotton candy. She said it was a reminder that since the race never ends, the winner is obviously the mouse.

Rat Race is set up in her room, which no one has entered since her death. But I want the diorama for my desk. It feels a little like an inheritance.

A notification pops up on my phone. A message from my lung sister.

Hi, sorry for the late reply. While I'm grateful for my new lungs, I don't want to meet. I don't want to meet you. It would be looking backward, and I only want to move forward. You can come and cheer me on at this year's Transplant Games though. I'll be competing in four events. Please don't contact me again.

She sounds like a rat. I look up the Transplant Games. They're in Toronto this fall. I find it hard to believe that you can have new lungs swapped in and be racing in four or five months. Sounds like she received both of Minnie's lungs, a double transplant. That means one less person around the campfire in my movie.

On the outline of Minnie, I shade in the lungs a purple color, the liver yellow—because that's the way it's headed at this point—and decide to hold off on a color for the heart. My lung sister's comments keep running through my mind. My phone pings. Another Instagram post by Mothman. A monarch butterfly perched on a bloom of dozens of small purple flowers. **Contrast is the color of life. #goodday**

But it's not the color of life for me. On my floor, Minnie's outline is purple, brown and yellow. The hues are faded and bleed into each other. I try to summon an actual image of my sister and can't, which sends a chill down my spine.

I slip my VR headset over my eyes and move into the center of my room, away from objects. Behind me two sensors track the headset. In front of me wires trail from my headset to the computer. It's pretty easy to become disoriented when using the goggles, but there's little left in my room to hit. I load an old file. Suddenly I'm in our garage, Minnie's former workshop. As my sister manifests, I relax. Minnie's then-dyed-silver hair glints beneath incandescent bulbs. She is skinning a skunk.

I smile, remembering that the garage still smells a little of skunk and the baking powder she used to wash the pelt again and again. On the workbench are her tools—wire cutters for the armature that holds the shape of the creature, a bag of cotton balls to fill it out, pliers, scalpels, a box with different jaw sets and compartments for glass eyeballs (Minnie had a dream of one day being able to use tiger's-eyes or star sapphires), needle and thread, and pins stuck in a pin cushion shaped like a strawberry.

There's the steady *snip, snip* of scissors as she works. The armature strapped with cotton and wrapped in string gives a hint of her plans, wire front legs pointing up, snout dipping down, as if preparing for a high dive. On shelves lined with spools of different thread and wires of various gauges, mice inspect her progress with their beady eyes—one uses glasses, another peers through a tiny telescope that she fashioned using a jeweler's loop. The camera has captured dust motes swirling, as if a touch of magic dances in the warmth as she brings her corpses to a form of life. In the corner, near her airbrush and paints, the skunk's diving platform dries.

My dad stands as far away as possible from her, with his back pressed up against a cupboard filled with old paint cans.

"Dad, don't be so crazy," Minnie says, responding to some question he's asked. "If I don't do this, then the street cleaners just scoop the skunk off the road and throw it in the garbage. I'm not hurting anything. In some ways, we both do the same job. You take vegetables and make them look like meat. I take a hide and make it look alive again."

"How's that the same?" He shakes his head. "What if what you're doing becomes a trend? People will hunt skunks, and for what? To put them...onstage. As trophies!"

"Onstage." She laughs. "Do you really think taxidermy will ever be cool?"

He shrugs. "I didn't think beards would be cool." He scratches at his.

"Yeah, Dad, you're so cool." She rolls her eyes so that her eyelids flutter. "Left on the road, an animal would be run over and over and over again. Then thrown in the landfill beneath garbage. Let me explain it another way. A hunter celebrates the kill. If it's not for food, then it's a trophy. Proof of his or her superiority. I'm not into that. I celebrate the life of the animal. I mount it to honor it. You are celebrating the vegetable to try to cut down on the killing of animals. It's the same dream."

This is how I remember her always explaining taxidermy. She honored the animal by making its death meaningful. Was I honoring her now with my video, animating her organs? How do we honor our dead? Hundreds of people came to the funeral. There was singing and speeches and slideshows. And then it was over. Our house was empty, our freezer full, our lives hollow.

"You honor the animal by making it do ballet?" my dad asks.

"Hey, a sculptor must find the form within the rock. Sometimes a badger wants to be a ballerina. And a cauliflower a sheep."

"A cauliflower sheep," he muses. "That's a pretty good idea!"

They burst into laughter, and, watching this in my room, I bite down on my hand to keep from crying. This was a lifetime ago.

"You should go on some of the taxidermy forums," she adds. "You'll see. These people really care about the animals."

I go cold.

I rip off the headset and wipe away my tears. I stagger at the sudden return to the bedroom, but my mind is focused on what my sister said. I've been looking in the wrong places for the organ recipients. I need to look for them on their forums.

Every disease, condition, disability and special-interest group has its own forum. To their members, these are identities, lifelines, surrogate families. I am part of a screenwriters' forum and VR forums. A couple of people have offered me technical pointers on how to do what I want to do for Minnie's video.

If I can find the right forum, maybe I can find a thread where someone has mentioned receiving an organ from my sister.

Within a few minutes I'm a member of a diabetes forum, and I've learned a lot about kidney failure. After navigating through several kidney-disease subforums, I land on one that discusses transplants. I scan for a congratulations thread and find it easily.

Place your good news here! reads the thread title.

A member who goes by the profile name Insulin Junkie has posted about receiving a new kidney only days after my sister died. She thanks members of the Mississauga Hospital Transplant Team—that's pretty close. It's a good one, she brags, a teenage organ. Will last my lifetime!

I have her.

Now I only need her address. Asking directly hasn't worked well so far, and I'm reluctant to do it here, but the woman has offered to speak to anyone about the experience.

I'd love to discuss the whole process. Would you mind? I post.

Her response is immediate. **Of course! When did you go on the list?**

She naturally assumes that I'm prepping for an operation too, and I let the assumption slide. If she knew the truth, she might not want to talk to me, but that doesn't mean she shouldn't.

Instead I write, **The place you had your transplant is pretty close to me. Could we meet in person?**

Her next message isn't on the forum—it's through the in-forum email.

We make a date for tomorrow.

On Minnie's outline I lightly trace a kidney in green for "go."

My phone buzzes.

A text. **Can I come over?**

I don't recognize the number. **Who are you?**

Kidney friend.

I look back to the laptop screen, stunned and confused, but then glance at the outline of Minnie. Of course. She has *two* kidneys. Someone found *me*! Yes, please.

I'm at your door.

I grin. Now *this* is a good day. I race to the door and throw it open.

NINE

On the steps is an Asian-looking guy a little older than me. He wears a thin yellow tie over an Iron Man T-shirt and black, ripped jeans. His arms are in the air as if he's cheering at a concert.

"I'm Dennis," he says. "I'm alive!"

I blink and say, "Hi, Dennis. I'm Emmitt." He looks over my shoulder and down the hall. "Come on in?" I ask.

"I will!" He lowers his arms and leaps past me into the house. "I'm so sorry about your sister. So sorry." He's clearly trying to tamp down his joy as best he can. "But I'm so happy to meet you."

"You sure seem happy."

Dennis swallows, eyes widening. "But I'm sorry too."

"I got it," I say.

He breaks back into a grin. "When you are almost dead and then suddenly not dead, so sick you cannot move and then can dance, when there is nothing in front of you and then…" His hand sweeps the world behind him. "Everything."

A peculiar kind of happiness-sadness wells in my chest. Pride in my sister for having done this.

"It makes everything taste better, smell better, sound better. Better than I ever remembered before I got sick." His lips twist in a wry smile. "Especially out of the hospital, huh?" He doesn't wait for an answer, barreling on. "I want to know everything about your sister. *Everything*. Where do we start?"

I suddenly feel as though he's on the wrong side of the threshold. That I've let something dangerous into the house.

He must read it in my face. "Oh, dude, I'm sorry. I talk too much. It's just…" His hands drift back toward the ceiling. "I'm *alive*."

"Come on in," I say again, a bit more welcoming now. We move farther down the hall, and after I place a finger to my lips, we creep past the living room where the television flickers. A soap-opera rerun.

"That your mom? *Her* mom?" Dennis asks with a note of reverence, like we're in the White House and have caught a glimpse of the president's family.

I nod, and Dennis takes off his ballcap and then steps toward her. I tap him on the shoulder and shake my head. "Not now," I say. "She's not feeling well."

He cranes his neck and replies, "She's sooo beautiful."

Into my mind flashes my mother the day after last tax season, greeting me at the door, gripping my hands hard and pulling me into a wild, spinning dance. It's an accountant's happiest day of the year. Her face is a crazy, grinning blur. Beautiful.

It hurts. Dennis is who I'd hoped for. Someone so filled with gratitude it explodes from him, but now that he's here, I feel it's too much too soon. Too much for my mom.

I tug Dennis toward my bedroom.

"That's weird." Dennis points down at Outline Minnie. "What's that for?"

"I'm checking off the organ recipients I find. You're one of the kidneys."

"The one on the right," he says with certainty. "And the pancreas too. Still weird."

"Sure. Now that I've found you, I can color you in. What color do you want?"

"Orange, of course!" He laughs wildly, catches himself and whispers, "I wonder who my kidney twin is! I'd love to meet them. There should be a transplant twin day, where we all get together and show our scars and tell stories of what we've done since."

"Maybe, yeah." Dennis is a bit odd. "How'd you find me anyway?" I ask.

"I saw your post but didn't want to just send back a message. I had to trace you using a fifth-grade class photo an old friend of yours posted. I called your elementary school to get your address, but of course they're closed for the summer, so I had to pretend to be a friend of yours from camp—Camp Kawabi? You went there a few years back. They gave it to me after hearing you'd lost your sister. They send condolences, FYI. Even though it was an old address, it wasn't too hard to follow your last move—holy crap, is that a virtual-reality rig?" He picks up the headset and looks at me pleadingly. "Can I?"

"I tell you what," I say. His eyes shine. "I'll let you use it if you'll let me film you. With any luck, you'll eventually be able to meet Minnie and all of your other organ…twins."

"Yes! Hook me up."

Carefully, like he's setting down a breakable vase, he eases the headset back onto my desk. "Whoa! Are those real?"

He's poking at the diorama. Somebody needs to tie this guy down. "Yup."

"That's gross."

"Pretty much."

"But neat."

Maybe it's because he's a great excuse, or maybe it's because his energy is contagious and I've been wanting to do this for weeks, I don't know, but I say, "My sister used to make them. Do you want to see more?"

His expression says he does. I pad back down the hallway, listening for the TV. I motion for Dennis to follow and cross to my sister's room. The door's closed but not locked.

I step inside. Beneath the dust of closure lies the musk of animal fur, talcum powder and potpourri.

"It's like a dollhouse," Dennis says.

Closing the door behind me, I put my finger to my lips again. Dennis nods. It's more than a dollhouse. The walls are filled with shelves, each subdivided into rooms and cut with holes between to allow for stairs, ladders and ropes that drop into dungeons. It's a world—or many worlds. On the top shelf a skunk dives from a cloud perch down into a blue lake with mice in rowboats, one on a Jet Ski, another kitesurfing. Beneath that lake water cascades in a fall of blue streamers into an underground cavern where a cat with seven mice heads lurks. In another scene squirrels shop at a supermarket called Walnuts, their baskets full of them. And in another a ladder leads to a sewer with red-eyed rats.

"I love her," Dennis says.

"My mom built the shelves," I reply. "At least initially, and then Minnie…"

Minnie took over. She filled the room. Filled every room.

"Sooo much detail." Dennis inspects the burrows of rabbits on a farm. "Oh my god." He pokes at a toy combine that has cleared a strip of dried grass made to look like wheat. "Is that…?"

"Yup, that's Chip," I say and can't help but smile. "That was Minnie's first-ever chipmunk."

Contorted in the tines of the combine's blades lies a mangled chipmunk.

"Whoa. Dark, man."

I laugh. "She had a boyfriend who dumped her, and on the way home she found this little guy in the gutter."

"Oh, and was the ex-boyfriend's name—?"

"You got it."

"Chip."

We both burst out laughing.

The door crashes wide open, rattling the tiered shelves

of arrangements. In the doorway stands my mom. Her hair hangs in clumps, partway to dreadlocks. This is the most movement I've seen from her in weeks. "What are you doing in here?" she yells.

I dash in front of Dennis as if to shield him. "Mom, Dennis here wanted to know about Minnie. He got one of her kidneys and her pancreas."

"I heard laughing. How can you laugh?" Her fingers on the doorjamb whiten. "Get out! Get *out*!"

She drops to her knees, blocking our exit. Dennis glances to me for help and then to the windows. I take him by the elbow, and we shuffle past her tensely, as if she might tackle us. But my mom's shaking and sobbing.

"Sorry," Dennis says as he tiptoes by her. "I'm sorry."

My mom replies, "I can't do it. I can't."

I let Dennis out the front door without another word. We'll do the film another time.

When I return my mom's already back on the couch, still crying. I want to apologize, explain that we got carried away. That we weren't laughing at Minnie. Her bedroom door is shut now. In my room I try to quell the panic by listing my tasks. I call my liver brother. Then I text Dennis an apology and ask that he listen to Metallica at 9:00 p.m. We still need to do the video, I add, to which he replies, Okay, but maybe not at your house, okay?

I pick up my copy of *Dune* and turn to page one, getting a head start. On my phone I watch the music video for "Nothing Else Matters." I wonder if my heart sister has ever seen it. The camaraderie of the band looks like what Minnie and I once shared. It's like a punch in the gut.

TEN

efore the sun is up, I hear the front door slam. My dad on his way to work. I roll over, fall back to sleep and don't throw off my covers until past ten o'clock. I rub my bleary eyes. Last night I read two hundred pages of *Dune* before nodding off. Had my heart sister caught up? Had we been reading the exact same page, same paragraph—word, even—for a moment? Were we in sync?

I pull on a pair of pants.

A note on the kitchen counter from my dad says he'll be late tonight. It's the same note from a few days ago that he's pulled from the recycling.

The sink brims with dishes. The couch is empty. I turn unthinkingly toward Minnie's room, to the person I've always turned to, whether for help or to share a laugh. But she's gone. I can only do my best to resuscitate her spirit.

I text Dennis and ask if he has time for his film shoot, to which I receive sixteen different emojis, all different forms of happiness. And then: **How about my place?**

I can't blame him for wanting to change the location of the set after his interaction with my mom. He lives only a mile from where I'm going to meet with Insulin Junkie. I agree to shoot at his apartment in a half hour. I check to see if my mom needs anything. The dim light of her room drains the morning's enthusiasm and sends me back to wash the dishes before leaving.

The streetcars run on time, but when I hop off, police-cruiser lights flash at a nearby intersection. I check my phone. The directions lead me back past the crowd of onlookers.

I swallow bile at the thought of someone else losing a sister, a mother, a friend. As I near, a break in the onlookers reveals a car straddling the pedestrian crosswalk. Heat burns through me, making it difficult to think. Each step toward the scene grows more difficult. An ambulance arrives. I look quickly at it and then away. A mistake. The scene is fresh. One car. One draped body. *Head injuries make great donors.* But I know it's already too late for a donation—the donor must die in hospital to qualify. Does that make this easier or harder? I stride away, head turned, and knock into a bystander.

"Sorry," I say and hurry down a side street to avoid the entire gawking nightmare of shattered bones and broken lives. I'm breathing hard, the detour taking me well off track. I'm late as I trudge the final steps to Dennis's apartment, hefting my bag.

Dennis lives in a walk-up above a Starbucks. Paint peels from the white front door that opens without a key. Flyers are strewn across the tiny entranceway and beneath two mailboxes with signs that read *NO KEY, please leave mail on floor.* The mailboxes are stuffed anyway. Before my heart sister, I could count on one hand the number of interactions I'd had in the form of a letter.

I hammer on the door of apartment B.

Dennis throws it open. "Welcome to my place!"

The inside is a bit like Neo's apartment in the movie *The Matrix.* A desk covered in computer gear. Hard drives everywhere. DVDs used like coasters for cans of Coke or dangling from window frames to catch the light and cast arcs of rainbows that remind me of raven feathers. A mattress strewn with clothes. A sink full of dishes. It stinks. But then I remember that this is a guy who, up until a couple of months ago, was dying of kidney failure. It's impressive he was able to live alone at all. But finding a place to set up will be a challenge.

"I love it here!" says Dennis.

I grin.

"You're amazing," I say. I believe it. "Sorry I'm late. Car accident. Not me, but—"

He beams. "I cleared an area for the video."

I can't tell. "I'll need a corner."

Dennis retrieves a broom from the closet and starts sweeping dust balls. I relax in the mess. "Let's do this," I say.

EXT. CAMPFIRE - NIGHT

Around the campfire, MINNIE (16) sits with DENNIS (early 20s). She has her guitar across her knees and plucks absently at the strings without realizing she's doing it. She grins at him, face aglow, sparks flying into the night.

                    MINNIE
          What's your name?

                    DENNIS
          Dennis.

                    MINNIE
          If you were an animal,
          what would you be?

                    DENNIS
          I was just thinking
          about this!

    "Right, because everyone has the answer on the tip of their tongue," I say.

                    DENNIS
          I do! An orangutan.

With long orange
dreads.
         (nodding)
My mom was Chinese.
Indonesian, from
Sumatra. Fled here
after the riots when
her parents' property
was stolen. Orangutans
were her favorite
animals.

              MINNIE
If I were to put you
in a diorama, what
would it look like?

              DENNIS
Video games kept me
sane while I was on
the list, during all
the dialysis. I really
didn't think I was
going to make it off
the transplant list.
Maybe I'd be in a
video game. No...wait...

Dennis shakes a hand at Minnie.

DENNIS (CONT'D)
I can do better. See,
I was a barista too.
An amazing one. I
love coffee. Foam so
smooth. My diorama
would have a spotlight
on me. Stars whipping
past. As I make a
cappuccino.

Dennis's hand shakes again.

DENNIS (CONT'D)
Wait. I'm redefining,
right? I don't know.
I've been sick for so
long, that was what I
had become. The best
part about this is
I can finally define
myself without being
defined by illness.
Maybe there's just
this spotlight, and a
director person
just said, "Action!"

MINNIE
Cool. What would other

people put in your
diorama?

DENNIS
Whoa. You know what?
I bet I'd be this sick
gamer to them. They
don't know me, not
physically. The ones
who did, they'd see me
as a kid in a hospital
bed. But that's over.

MINNIE
How can you make the
diorama better?

Dennis's chin tilts upward.

DENNIS
Orangutan me is gonna
hang from the tree
branches and swing and
collect durian fruit or
termites or whatever
they eat and use my
super-amazing fingers
to code even faster.
And when I'm done, I'm
gonna donate my organs!

```
And if I don't die when
they're still useful,
I'll give money,
because every moment
from here on out I owe
to the kind stranger
who gave their organs
to me. I owe you.


Dennis laughs.


His eyes sparkle with humor,
and Minnie grins back.


                        FADE OUT.
```

"That was awesome," I say when we're done.

Dennis keeps nodding and nodding. "Orangutan me thinks everything is awesome."

"Sorry you were sick for so long," I say.

He shrugs. "Nothing I could do about it."

"I worked in a coffee shop too," I say. We grin at each other for a moment. "Thanks for this, but I gotta run. I've got a date with your kidney twin."

"Really?" He launches from where he is kneeling on the floor. "I'm coming!"

"Sorry, but she doesn't even really know I'm her kidney brother."

Dennis grimaces and picks at a crust of something staining his shirt. "So how did you set it up?"

"She thinks I'm on the transplant list. That I'm nervous about the operation. I didn't tell her that, but I did let her assume it. I only asked to meet."

Dennis's bouncy eagerness evaporates. Sticky silence takes its place. "You really need this video, huh?"

"My parents do," I say.

He considers another moment and says, "Okay. Well, good luck, man. Let me know how it goes."

I leave Dennis's apartment feeling unsettled, the strap of the messenger bag biting hungrily into my shoulder. The emergency vehicles have left the accident scene now, and I reach the coffee shop in good time. The whole way there I had the feeling that someone was watching me, but every time I turned around, there was no one to be found.

ELEVEN

I'd imagined someone with the profile name Insulin Junkie to look different than the older woman I see sipping a latte. She's dressed like a grandmother but moves with the quick, sure movements of someone twenty years younger. I know her by the heavy jade earrings she said she'd be wearing, which drag down her earlobes.

"Soy, half decaf, one pump vanilla, extra hot," I say, spotting the code on the side of her cup.

Her eyes light up. "Why, yes, it is!"

"Best job I ever had, but then they had a management change, and it became all about pushing drinks."

"You must be my coffee date," she says. "My name's Eileen."

"Emmitt." I shake her hand before sitting down.

"You look well," she says.

"Thanks, I feel…pretty good."

"You're lucky. I only made the transplant list after the doctors ran out of places to put my dialysis catheter," she explains, her eyes drifting to my neck and my covered arms. *Is she looking for my port?* "With so long a list and so few kidneys available, they usually wait until you're nine-tenths dead. I had weeks to live. Normally they don't give someone my age an organ from someone so young. Most people aren't so lucky."

I can tell she's suggesting I probably won't be. Her watery blue eyes consider mine.

"Lucky you," I say.

"So. What would you like to know?"

The longer I wait to explain why I'm really here, the more this is going to hurt. "Now that you have a new kidney, what will change?" I dig myself in deeper.

Eileen's eyes widen and take on a faraway look that I'm beginning to recognize.

"Dialysis is like a tether. Every two days for me. Four hours I was plugged into a machine. What can you do when every two days you're dragged back to the hospital for a blood scrubbing? What will I do now that I don't have any more dialysis? Travel, golf, bridge…romance!" She shakes her head as if the thought of options is too much. "But then, you'd know all about this."

I swallow and nod. "I'm doing a film project on organ recipients. Would you mind being in it?"

"No, oh no, I don't think I should be in front of a camera." When she cups the bottom of her hair in her palm and primps, I know I can persuade her.

"It would be for donors. A sort of thank-you," I say.

"Donors don't need thank-yous," Eileen says with a sad smile. "Do they?"

She's saying this because they're dead, and I understand, even if I disagree. "For their families. Do you know anything else about your donor?"

She shrugs and quirks her lips in a way that suggests it really doesn't matter. "I'm not sure I would want to know even if I could."

"Why's that?" I feel myself shift forward to the edge of my seat and try to relax.

"What if I don't like who the person was? Now I have them inside of me."

"But they could have been wonderful."

"Or a serial killer. And who's to say their other organs aren't being implanted in serial killers?"

"What—" I begin, but she's staring at the ceiling, chattering away.

"Hopefully they'll soon be able to 3-D print them. And they can be tailor-made for us. So we don't have to worry so much."

"I'm not sure I understand what you mean." I place my hand on her arm, and she stares at it like it's a knife. I draw away.

Eileen's eyes are clear and firm as she faces me. "All I'm saying, dear, is that it's easier not to know where it came from. You never know..." She looks around and then leans right over the table. "It's inside of me. You'll understand when it's someone else inside of you."

I am starting to understand. But I have to be sure. "So are you saying you don't want to know if your kidney came from someone with, say, a different race or religion?"

Her face says it all. My butt slides to the back of my chair.

She shifts back too. "I didn't say that. Listen, I offered to meet with you. To tell you about the drawbacks, the immunosuppressants, the fact that the organ won't last forever, to be careful what you wish for. You can live on dialysis for a long time."

I don't want to film her.

"I know who your donor was," I say.

Eileen squints at me.

"Yeah, the film is about everyone who received his organs. I'm researching."

Her jaw sets, bracing. "It's supposed to be anonymous."

"I found you, didn't I?"

"Well, I don't want to know. I also have a right to privacy."

"He's a black Muslim named Mohammed."

She pales and clenches her hands.

"But don't worry. His family were professionals before they had to flee Ethiopia. Good genes. It's a first-class kidney you've got. It had been accepted to medical school."

I am enjoying the horror on her face far too much. I know this is wrong, but I can't help myself.

Out of the corner of my eye, I spot Dennis. He's sitting at a table in the corner. He must have followed me. When I catch his eye, he grins and waves so hard that his chair rocks back and forth. He must take my surprise as an open invitation, because he rushes over, hand outstretched. Eileen's mouth is hanging open. Before she can speak, Dennis is at our table.

"Are you my kidney twin?" Dennis says. "We're family!"

I don't know whether to laugh or cry. But I'm pretty sure we're all about to get what we deserve.

TWELVE

"What is going on?" Eileen demands.

Dennis pumps her limp hand as he explains, "If you have Emmitt's sister's kidney and I have the other one, you're my organ twin! Listen, can we assume I received the one on the right? Please?"

Eileen yanks her hand away and wipes it on her blouse. "His sister." She turns to me. "You lied."

"A white lie," I say with a smirk.

She looks like I struck her. Her shaking hands cause some of her latte to spill across the table.

"She's not my kidney twin?" Dennis asks.

"No, she is, but I think she'd rather not be."

Eileen reddens and grabs her purse.

"I thought I was being helpful," she says as she stands. "And then you attacked me."

I don't reply. Everyone in the coffee shop is listening now.

"Is she going to be in our movie?" Dennis asks in a

hushed tone, obviously still confused.

"No," she replies through gritted teeth.

"Why not?" Dennis cries. "All of us are in it, and Emmitt asks these tough questions about, well, I guess they're really about who we were and who we are now, now that the transplant is changing us. It's important."

"Nothing in me is changing." Eileen laughs without humor.

"Except my sister's kidney," I say. "It's not like switching batteries."

Her face twists, becoming ugly and gnarled.

"Your sister died, and I was lucky enough that she'd registered to allow the doctors to do with her body as they pleased after she was dead. After you're dead, you're owed nothing."

Dennis shakes his head. "She didn't have to register for organ donation."

"No one should need to register," she says.

"But they do," I reply.

"I don't think your sister was thinking about me when she signed up."

"I have to agree there," Dennis replies.

Eileen turns her back to us and strides for the door.

I clench my hands into fists. I'm enraged that my sister saved this woman's life. And she doesn't seem to care. What would Minnie want me to say?

"You're wrong, Eileen," I call. She pauses with her hand against the glass door. The other patrons swing their gazes from me to Eileen and then back to me. "My sister was a taxidermist. She took dead things and stuffed life into them. You're like a dead thing, and now you've had life stuffed into you. I bet you can do better. That's all my sister would have asked. You just haven't realized how truly lucky you are. Not yet."

Eileen pushes through the door. It slams behind her.

Dennis looks at me. "I don't think she wants to be in your movie."

"Nope."

"Sorry I crashed your party."

"It had already crashed."

"People like her make organ donation the ultimate gift."

"You can't be serious," I say. "That woman is horrible."

"No, I am serious! You're giving to strangers. No strings attached. It's something that bonds everyone. Anyone can give. Anyone can receive. Shows we're all in this together. Universal love."

"I guess."

"What are you going to do now?"

I slump back in my chair at the sloppy table. So far my sister's organs have gone to a killer, a drunk, a racist and—Dennis leans down and sucks up some of the latte pooling on the table surface—Dennis. I have to find my heart sister. She's the only way I can redeem the video project.

"I need to find the person who received Minnie's heart," I say.

"Hospital would have the record," Dennis says, wiping his mouth.

"But the hospital won't give the record to me."

"Then hack them. Hey, did you know that vanilla flavoring used to come from beaver butts?"

"I'm not hacking a hospital." I snort. "Sorry about your kidney twin being such a jerk."

"I guess we know who the evil kidney twin is, huh?"

A staff member sweeps in with a cloth to mop up the table.

"I'm not sure there are always evil and good twins, but I'd agree for sure that one twin can be better than the other," I reply.

We sit in silence for a moment.

"What are we listening to tonight? What music?" Dennis finally asks. "Please, no more heavy metal."

"Your call," I say.

"Blackpink." When I don't respond, he adds, "K-pop."

"Okay then."

"Nine o'clock," he says.

On the streetcar home, the location of the accident flashes past, all clear, like it never happened. It bothers me how Eileen implied that without Minnie she'd still be alive, just with someone else's kidney. That's not true. People on the transplant list die every day. What are the chances that I will affect someone's life as profoundly as Minnie has? The tattoo on my shoulder gives a twinge of pain, and I flash back to the twitch of Minnie's hands before shaking my head of these thoughts.

As I approach the cracked concrete of our doorstep, I spot the corner of an envelope sticking out from

the mailbox. My pace quickens. I vault up the steps.
I grab the envelope and tear it open.

Dear Heart Brother,

I sink to the stair to read in the afternoon sun.

> *Hooray! Now we are connected. Thank you for
> writing, but how about giving a girl something to work
> with? And maybe ease into the questions, huh?*
> *What's it like to have someone's heart in my chest?
> It's a strange thing. Imagine holding a little red bird
> in your hands that wants to fly away and you have to
> keep your hands closed but loose enough that the bird
> can breathe. You're right, though—it's also like I'm
> Iron Man and someone has placed a great and powerful
> responsibility in me. But, my heart brother, be careful not
> to foist your own ideals on others, right? That's not cool.*

I make a mental note to be more gentle with Joey.
But Eileen? My anger at her feels pretty justified.

> *Does the donor family have any rights? I dunno.
> I honestly think we should have more donors. That it
> shouldn't be such a scarce resource. If I was a candidate,
> I'd be a donor (I'm on way too many drugs for anyone to
> want my organs, but I've signed up just in case). I know
> what it means to be alive because someone registered for
> organ donation and talked to their family about it. It's
> strange because it's the most powerful thing you can do,*

and it costs you absolutely nothing. Yet so many people don't bother. What are families planning on doing with the organs? The dead person can't use them anymore, and who doesn't want to save a life doing something that costs nothing?

You're a donor, right? You must be.

Hot guilt flushes through me, but I shelve it for later.

I saw your "spelling mistakes," by the way. I'm sorry, but I don't want to meet you.

"What?" I look to the sky. *What?* Why not? How can I finish without her? Anger and frustration press at the side of my head. "But you're my heart sister," I say to the page. "You *have* to." I read on, hoping for understanding.

I have my reasons. But please DON'T STOP WRITING! It doesn't mean I don't want to know more about you and your sister. Here's an easy question for you—this is how you ease into things, buddy—do you want to be famous?

But you asked me a tough question too. So here's one for you. What's it like to lose your sister? I'm sorry.

I love you,

Heart Sis

With a lump in my throat, I press the letter to my chest. She's the star of my video. I imagine her. Blond— no, brown hair cascading in the moonlight, glowing almost. It's her eyes that matter most to me. Pools of shimmering compassion. She's the one who could help my mother. She sounds amazing. But why wouldn't she want to meet us? *Maybe she does.*

Was her comment a misdirection for the benefit of the censors, telling *me* to look for a code? I search her note. I try the first letters of sentences, then words. I can't find any spelling errors or other symbols that might point to a cipher. Nothing.

What's the problem with meeting me? And if the code won't do it, then what will?

I fold the note and slip it into my pocket.

After I shut the door to the house, it takes several long moments for my eyes to adjust to the dark hallway.

"Mom?" I ask. The TV is off. The curtains are drawn. "Mom?"

A chill washes over me. I switch on the hall light.

The couch is empty. No note from her in the kitchen, my note untouched. The dishes are dry but still out. I rush to my bedroom. The hall bathroom is empty. I slink to my parents' bedroom door. It's late afternoon. Outside, chimneys filter the final rays of sunlight. She should be up.

I knock.

No answer.

I ease open the door.

There she is, buried in blankets. "Mom?" I ask gently.

Nothing.

"Mom!"

When her head lifts, I tremble with relief.

"Mom, it's so late. What's happening? Did you even get out of bed today?"

Her head sags back on the pillow.

I reach her bed, and as I slide onto the side of the mattress, she turns her face away. "Mom, you have to get up. You have to keep moving."

She doesn't move.

"No, Mom, come on."

A moan escapes her lips. "Minnie wasn't the only one who died, Emmitt. I did too. All the hopes and dreams I had imagined for her. All that she knew of me. The memories that we had shared. I held on to those things because they were ours. Things she remembered for me, like when the next episode of our favorite show would drop, how to make Grandma's ginger cookies—I don't even know your grandfather's birthday. These things she knew for me. I don't know how to live without that part of me."

Anger stirs in my belly. What can I say to her? That my loss is greater? That she has no idea what it's like to lose your twin—can't ever know? Because Minnie might have remembered things for my mom, but she was my secret keeper, my dream bearer. I know Minnie only watched those shows because they were our mother's favorite—not Minnie's— and she had everyone's birthday scheduled in her phone. What do I tell my mom? It's an odd notion that we need other people to remember stuff for us. That somehow their death is our death or the death of a piece of us. It frustrates me. Like the laundry does. The cooking. The fact that everyone else is up and moving forward except her.

"I understand," I say. Even though I don't. Not really.

"I have to let those things go too. My memories of her," she adds. "Let them go or drown in them. But I can't. I want to be drowned in them."

I can't keep the words in anymore. "You don't think we all do, Mom?" I demand. "You don't think *I* want to hide in a corner?"

Her head rocks from side to side, not wanting to hear, but she needs to hear it.

"You're being selfish," I say.

She buries her head in her comforter.

"Get up!" I stand over her, quaking.

The comforter heaves with her sobs. I crumble to my knees.

"Mom, I'm sorry," I say. "I know. I'm only trying."

She cries harder.

I ease back the cover. Her face is scrunched *tight* tight.

I run my hand over my mother's forehead, like she used to do for me years ago. How I've wished over these last weeks that she would do it for me again. I have nothing more to say. All I can think is, How do I find my heart sister? She's all we have left of Minnie.

How do I hack a hospital?

THIRTEEN

I wake up and realize Dennis texted me several times
last night when I was supposed to be rocking out to
K-pop. It's a good thing I set my alarm for calling Joey
to ask him the three questions, or I would have missed
that too.

Sorry, Dennis. I had a rough night, I text, holding
up a hand to block the sunlight streaming through my
blinds.

He replies with a poop emoji, then: Anything I can
help with?

You know how you talked about hacking the
hospital to access medical records?

There's a long pause.

Finally: If she's your heart sister, does that make
her my heart cousin?

I'm not sure.

That would be cool. Or maybe second cousin
once removed. When I don't reply, he adds, Get it?

'Cause the organ is removed? Too early? Probably too early.

Hospital. Hack. How? I don't have time for this.

This time it's a full minute before Dennis answers.

Hospitals sometime still have ancient X-ray and CAT-scan equipment and software that hasn't been updated for years. So we could try to get in that way. Or we could do some spear phishing to get someone's user ID and password. Like, 'Hi, Dr. Jean, this is Hans in IT. We've had a breach using your ID 6254. To reset your password,' yada yada. But probably the easiest way is how I tracked you down.

Easiest, please, I text. Unlike Dennis, I keep my texts short. More waiting. I kick off my covers and pull on yesterday's jeans and T-shirt while I watch the three little dots.

Except a hospital will be tougher. It'll take research. Go to the hospital, figure out how it operates, find a flaw in their security processes, and use it against them.

I can't believe I once thought we might not get along. My challenge is keeping up with the guy. Still, as smart as he is, I really don't want to return to the hospital. I'm also positive they don't want me back. I'm surprised they didn't ban me.

Minnie's PICU doctor was Dr. Lebow. Middle-aged, all business and the bedside manner of a turnip. The day after the accident, without so much as a *hey, how is everyone doing?* she had invited in the organ coordinator from the transplant team. This guy had immediately launched into his spiel. "We see Minnie is registered as an organ donor and would like to reaffirm the family's desire to donate her organs. Do I have your—"

But I was already moving. I threw myself on top of Minnie and then craned my neck to give Lebow a death stare. "You. Will. Never. Touch. Her." The back of my throat burned. But Lebow didn't even blink.

The organ coordinator turned to my parents. "Consent. Do I have your consent?"

"How can she have registered? She's only sixteen," I said.

"Sixteen is the age of consent for organ donation. I know this isn't easy—"

"Can we have a moment?" my mom asked.

I learned later that my parents had already met with the coordinator and a social worker. But at the time, I turned my stare on my mother, who flinched. I wondered then if she had known.

Dr. Lebow hesitated, and I caught the longing look she cast at Minnie. Maybe in retrospect it was only her desire to help others, but at the time it seemed like the gaze of a greedy god. I wouldn't leave Minnie's side, already imagining going for a snack only to return and find the room empty.

"Touch her, and I'll kill you," I said as Dr. Lebow left the room with her sidekick.

I'm guessing people remember things like that, so I really want to avoid any run-ins with Dr. Lebow.

That's the easiest? I ask Dennis.

Yep, it's called social engineering. Can I come? I can help.

I hesitate. I think this is something I have to do on my own, Dennis.

Maybe I can run interference? Start a flash mob? I know! If I start a fire in a—

I'll ask if I need help. I promise.

I take his lack of a response as acceptance.

I pack a couple of peanut-butter sandwiches. The baggie of food seems insufficient, considering my mission. Where's my hacking kit? What the hell am I thinking? *Don't think. Thinking is the enemy.* Maybe I should bring Dennis. But what I don't want is attention, and Dennis is an attention magnet.

I head for the subway. The line runs right past the hospital where my sister died. I'm outside of its glass-enclosed entry inside twenty minutes. My sister was only here for three days, two on life support and then another as one of the living dead while they prepared to recover her organs. I struggled with that part.

I wasn't there when the doctor finally declared Minnie dead, but I was there *before* they went in to conduct the final test, and I was there *after* the testing. The only difference between those times was the doctor's declaration. Before they went in there was hope, and after there was none. Intellectually I know it meant Minnie was dead long before the doctor knuckled her sternum or administered the apnea test, but at the time I was listening to my heart. My heart knew Minnie was still alive. Hope remained.

Afterward my dad took my mom home to get some sleep and a shower. I stayed.

"This is your last chance," I told Minnie. My eyes roved over her, searching for signs. "Are you pretending?"

I leaned my forehead to hers and opened myself to her thoughts, promising that if she pushed some animal, vegetable, number, letter—anything—to me, I'd fight for another day. But there was nothing. I couldn't even think of one myself.

"What are we going to do now?" I asked. "What am I going to do?"

I must have crashed, because I awoke when my parents returned. My head was groggy, my cheek holding the creases of Minnie's bedsheets. Dr. Lebow and two nurses stood solemnly by.

"It's time, son," my dad said.

My head snapped from my dad to my mother's tears, to the doctors and then to Minnie. *Minnie.* What had I dreamed? I tried to recall. Had she pushed anything to me? Had she spoken to me?

The nurses began fiddling with machines and wires, collecting the elements of Minnie's body's support. My heart raced.

"Just a little longer?" I asked.

"The others are here," my dad said.

The others. He meant the other surgeons, maybe some organ recipients.

"We love you, Minnie," my mother croaked.

Cords were bundled. Alarms switched off.

"I love you," my dad said and kissed her forehead.

Everyone looked to me, and my mind was blank. "I'll see you, Minnie. I'll see you again soon."

My parents gripped the edge of her bed as she was wheeled out, repeating "I love you" as they followed her to the elevator.

"I'll see you," I said. "I will."

They hollowed her out that night.

Now, as I stand before the impressive hospital entranceway built after someone donated a vast sum of money, someone who'd had a long, long life and time to think about how they could do some good in the world, I want nothing more than to retreat to my VR world and sit across from Minnie and listen to her play the ukulele.

A man shoulders past me, and I follow him inside.

The door thumps as it revolves, dumping me into the main lobby. Artificial light shines. A hospital is neither night nor day. It's an alien, self-contained world where someone is always awake. Where people share the worst or best days of their lives.

My sneakers know the way as I head to the PICU—the heart of the hospital's pain. Fluorescent lights stud the ceiling. People hustle in a steady stream up and down the hallways. I catch crying and laughter. A groan.

That's from the waiting room. At the entrance tension rides back up my spine as I recall what I'm here for. I am a would-be thief.

Several dozen people stand or sit in the chairs bordering the walls. One man shifts back and forth on his feet, as if rocking a baby. Another family clusters in a corner, a team trying to decide their next play. A team with a desperately small playbook. *Do we let the doctor operate? Or do we wait and see? What are the statistics? How many people survive the surgery? If they do, what's the quality of life?* Impossibilities.

These aren't choices. They are forks in a road full of switchbacks and sinkholes.

My blue plastic chair is occupied by a man staring dully at a TV silently delivering the news in black-and-white captions. Beside him a woman clutches his hand and leans against his shoulder. I'm unreasonably annoyed that they have my old spot. It should be labeled with a brass plaque: *Here Emmitt Highland heard news of his sister Minnie's death.* But then the room would be sheathed in brass, wouldn't it?

The waiting room relegates us all to childhood. In this room we are powerless. But we're also together. But today I feel like a voyeur. Maybe even a bit powerful.

I recognize a couple of people at the nursing station. They're talking to some friend or relative of a patient, and no one gives me a second glance. Muscles in my neck unravel. I've been here before. I can watch. My sandwich will be enough. I shuffle to sit with my back against the far wall.

I wait.

In the waiting room.

I could have selected another room, anywhere else in the hospital, but this place I understand. I'm a part of its walls and always will be. What am I watching for?

I need access to my sister's medical records. To the donor files. I'm here to see if I can find some kind of gap in their security. I don't really know how. I'll figure it out as I go.

A half door separates the waiting room from the nursing station and its bank of three computer screens. Behind the nursing station are double doors that swing out into the ward hallway. But the nursing station is busy. The computers with their access to medical records are all in use.

Suddenly the concept of trying to charm or dupe the nursing staff into handing over the info I need seems way more difficult than getting a doctor's password. Dennis had said an ID tag would be a big first step. Maybe I can grab one and then get the hell out of here.

Someone comes through the double doors. I go cold. It's Dr. Lebow. The same doctor who treated Minnie. Her facial expression is neutral as she scans the room for something or someone. I slide a *National Geographic* off a coffee table and open the magazine to hide my face. When she starts moving again, I track her and the swing of her ID tag that hangs from the pocket of her white lab coat. She looms over a huddled family.

There's a satisfying irony to choosing Dr. Lebow as my way into the hospital network. But how do I get the tag? Do I knock into her and grab it? Is it as simple and as difficult as that?

The family huddle opens for her. Hunched figures straighten. Eyes widen with fear. The ears of a nearby onlooker perk as he listens to the prognosis. I know what he's thinking. If this family has bad luck, there's a better chance his family won't. They can't all have bad luck, he is thinking. I know because that is what I thought. But everyone here has bad luck, everyone here in the purgatory of the PICU. It's not a zero-sum game, but if it were, this would be the unit that balances out the maternity ward.

I begin to stand but then hesitate. It can't be this easy, can it? Shouldn't I have to wait longer? But maybe this is my only chance. Maybe I'm just lucky. *Someone* must be lucky. I mean, on another street some driver isn't texting while at the wheel. Or they are driving extra slowly at night. Or they look up in time to hit the brakes.

I don't want to stay in the waiting room any longer than I need to.

What if I get caught?

No one knows what I'm doing. Caught for what? Bumping into a doctor? Loitering? Has anyone anywhere ever been charged with that?

I stand.

Dr. Lebow is speaking as I shuffle toward her. As I get closer, I hear, "Her white blood cell count is very high. It's indicative of an infection. An infection that we are attempting to treat with powerful antibiotics."

"How did this happen? It was only supposed to be a day surgery," someone replies.

"One in a thousand such surgeries have complications..."

Bad luck.

I try to tune it out, focus on the badge. If I approach the doctor from her right, I can make it look like I'm reaching for a *Time* magazine on the side table—its Person of the Year issue. On the cover is a man in a surgical mask. I'm being rude but not criminal. The alligator clip at the top of the badge will be simple enough to pry open. Voices rise in barely controlled anger. But eyes are not on me. They are on Dr. Lebow's expressionless face, and Dr. Lebow's eyes are on her hands and their expressive fingers that weave with her commentary. Fear darkens the borders of my vision. I tunnel toward the Person of the Year. The magazine is years old. *The Ebola Fighters*, says the headline. I'd forgotten about the Ebola outbreak. Will anyone remember my sister?

I need to be quick. Stumble, grab, apologize and then disappear.

Across the room a woman with nearly white hair watches. I'm acting strangely. I trip. My hand shoots out to steady myself against the doctor, but Dr. Lebow's already moving. Someone calls over the PA system. Between calls come bleats. An alarm. They have me. I snag the arm of a chair. Dr. Lebow runs toward the nursing station. I swing my hand out again to snatch at the flare of her lab coat, the swinging badge, but she's already past.

I missed, and I must run.

"Code blue, PICU, room 212," the speakers blare. "Code blue." *Bleep!*

Code blue. Not me, I realize. Someone else's bad luck.

The family members Dr. Lebow had been speaking to are shocked at the sudden departure of the doctor and my taking her place. I splutter and then point to the Ebola fighter. "I'd forgotten," I say. "It was so huge and scary, but I'd already forgotten."

I take the magazine and begin to wander back toward my seat, still uncertain if my cover is blown. I glance at the nursing station. It's empty. I check the time on my phone and wait. Counting.

One minute and forty-four seconds later, a nurse returns.

I have my security gap. And it's only ten o'clock. I do this today.

FOURTEEN

I go to the hospital entrance and text Dennis. **Do you know any doctors?**

His response is immediate. **You need help? 'Cause I am ready to help.**

I roll my eyes. **Yes, please. Doctors?**

I just had an organ transplant. I have way more doctors than friends.

Anyone you can text privately?

I have one cousin in medical school and an aunt who is a plastic surgeon. What's the question?

I need to know how to call a code in a hospital. A code that will have everyone running into the PICU. Theoretically.

Of course! I'll be back.

At a medical supply store, I purchase a white lab coat. Now I'm a doctor, maybe a junior doctor, if they have those. I google it. I can't be a medical student because they might not have access to records.

And then I see it. A medical resident.

I consider the stethoscopes, but they're really expensive. A lab coat should be all I need.

While I pay for the lab coat, Dennis texts me back. Just phone in the code and the location.

I don't need to give my name or badge number or say anything secret?

Code brown, PICU, room 218. There are phones all over the place.

Code brown.

He replies with a poop emoji. Just an example. But that room number is good. Farthest from the nursing station.

Dennis is a quick study. Okay, thanks.

Please, can I help? he asks again.

You have. I search on my phone's browser for hospital codes. I don't think a code brown will draw a big crowd, if it even exists. I need something big. Code white—violent patient. Or a code blue—no heartbeat. Either will bring everyone. And I'll find my heart sister.

I stand near the entrance to the PICU waiting room. The lab coat is rolled up in a plastic shopping bag. Fifteen minutes until noon. Lunchtime—that'll be when staffing is leanest. It'll be doubled up at shift change, when nurses hand over their patients. That's the time to avoid. A one-hour window. I have two minutes within a one-hour window.

I will call the code. Walk into the waiting room. Hop over the half door at the empty nursing station and search for Minerva Highland on their computer system.

I will take pictures of the medical record without reading it except to scan for mentions of organ recipients.

It's so James Bond—I love it. I only wish I was behind the lens and not playing the lead role.

A CCTV camera glints at the end of one hall, but I don't see any cameras in the corners of the waiting room. What's the criminal charge for calling a fake code? For stealing medical records? I don't want to know.

Despite the dry, cool air, sweat bursts from my pores. Twenty-five minutes remain until twelve fifteen. I can't stand here for that long without appearing suspicious, so I try other nursing stations, hoping to catch glimpses of computer screens. The more I understand the terminals, the better my chance of success. But anytime I walk to a computer, the person at it looks up and blinks at me expectantly. I need somewhere busy. Very busy.

I head for the emergency room.

Several people wear masks, whether to protect others from their germs or to protect themselves, I don't know. The coughing and sniffling are almost constant. Parents comfort wailing children. A guy holds one of his hands, wrapped in a bloody bandage, above his head. Two paramedics joke over an occupied gurney. A line of would-be patients waits at the triage station, but in a corner I spot a computer facing my direction. Someone in surgical scrubs consults it, then leaves. Another arrives. I fall into the triage line for a closer look.

The triage nurse focuses on the next emergency. At the computer in the corner, the orderly sways as he types, and I catch flashes of what's on the screen—one of those gray-and-white forms to fill in. From this distance I can't read the headings across the top, but I suspect I'll need to hit one, enter the name of the patient and bingo. When the orderly leaves, I exit the triage line and wander closer to the computer. But the orderly halts in mid-stride, lifts one hand and spins on his heel to face me. His eyes flick from the terminal to me and back. He takes a couple of steps, blocks the screen, hits *escape* a few times and then walks away. Now the screen is asking for login information.

That could be a problem.

I have another ten minutes to kill. I ask one of the mask wearers where they found the masks. A woman overhears and says, in a voice muffled by her mask, that the hospital drugstore carries them.

I thank her and head for the store. I am sure everyone knows what I'm up to and that I'm running out of time, even though I'm the one who set the arbitrary deadline. I nearly collide with a clown exiting the hospital's volunteer office.

"Oh ho, watch the feet!" the clown says, tapping the toes of his enormous red shoes together and laughing. The shoes slap down the hall as he walks away. While I was in the PICU with Minnie, a volunteer clown arrived at one point to cheer us up. He didn't stand a chance.

In the drugstore I ask about the surgical masks and buy a box of twenty.

At the entrance to the PICU, with a minute to spare, I shake out the lab coat and plunge my arms through the sleeves. Across the hall from the unit hangs a phone.

Goose bumps bubble up under the scratchy white sleeves. Lights shimmer. What am I doing? How did I reach this point? I glance over my shoulder and half expect to catch Minnie's wicked and mischievous grin of approval.

The surgical mask presses tight over my mouth and nose as I pull the elastic straps over my head, draw a deep breath and pick up the handset.

"Hospital operator," a dry voice answers.

"Code..." Which one was it? Oh, right. "Code Omega, PICU, room 218."

Omega. I can't help myself sometimes. It's code for catastrophic loss of blood.

"Sorry? I didn't catch the room number."

I pull down the mask. "Code Omega, PICU, room 218."

Almost immediately there's a bleep overhead. I hang up, and the PA announces the code. I stand frozen. The code is called again.

Move!

I hustle into the waiting room. Eyes swing to me, but the nursing station is empty. *Code Omega!* I nod at the people and stride officiously toward the nursing station, counting seconds. I make a face like I'm worried. I draw my phone as if it's a weapon and activate the camera function.

I leap over the half door, sit at a chair and scan the computer screen. This one requires a login. *Crap.* I try the next. Same problem. I have no time for this. Chair wheels squeal as I slide to the third one. It is still open.

I get a flash of Minnie's diorama of "Goldilocks and the Three Bears" where Goldilocks is a slavering rat with a blond wig, and Baby Bear is a mouse on the floor with his belly carved open. *Just Right* was the name of the scene. Minnie was an odd person.

I click on the search function and type my sister's name. There are three Minerva Highlands—I can hardly believe that—but I'm lucky with my first click. I'm snapping photos as I scroll my sister's massive medical record. Someone approaches the desk. I glance up, then back at the screen. The person tilts their head to the side, as if they're uncertain. It can't have been more than sixty seconds so far.

"I'll be right with you," I say.

At the bottom of the medical record are the linked records. I recognize Gerry and Dennis and Eileen. I have all the names. *Holy crap. I've done it.*

"Hold on. Let's see your ID," someone behind me orders.

I clear the screen.

The nurse's eyes burn.

FIFTEEN

"I'm a resident," I squeak.

"I know you." The nurse squints, mouth pinching. She stands with her fists tucked into her waist.

"I don't think so," I say, struggling to keep my back straight, as if I should be here. "I'm new."

Voices call out on the other side of the door, another nurse or doctor arriving, likely from the room with the fake code Omega. I have what I need. Now I need to get out of here.

"Who are you?" the nurse probes.

"I'm Dr. Mishma, new emerg resident," I say, panicking. "Heard the code—big one, Omega, blood everywhere, right? Well, I was checking to see if you needed help, saw you didn't and needed to pull up a record. The computers in the ER are so busy, know what I mean?" I stand, but the nurse doesn't budge. Her nose is at my chest.

The door opens.

"Who's this?" Dr. Lebow cocks her head at me. "Nurse?"

"Dr. Mishmash," the nurse replies with a droll tone. "Call security."

"Security? No, I-I-uh..." But there's nothing to be done.

I jump over the counter, but the nurse lunges and catches my arm. Fingers band my wrist. Dr. Lebow grabs for the phone. That's when someone in the waiting room starts screaming. A naked man with a backpack is grinning wildly. He begins dancing. Sort of. It's a combination of jumping jacks and the waltz. But done naked, which is all wrong.

I gasp.

It's Dennis. He starts singing what I suspect is a Blackpink song.

Dr. Lebow lowers the phone, and for a second the nurse's grip loosens. I tear free.

As I run, a call for security for me plays over the PA system, followed by a code white—for Dennis, I assume.

He sprints down the hall in the opposite direction of me, startling onlookers, and disappears around the corner.

I strip off my mask and lab coat and chuck them into a garbage can without breaking my stride. Scrambling down the stairwell flights, I hit a rear exit to the hospital, skipping out past some employees on a smoke break beside the garbage bins. I'm smiling as I reach the busy street, and then I start to laugh, even though my heart rams in my chest. My phone pings.

Run!

A cop car, lights flashing, screams around the corner. I cut across the road and into another hospital building, weaving through a crowded atrium to stand before an exit to a new street. I stay at the doorway until I'm sure the road is clear of police, draw a deep breath and stride onto a sidewalk glimmering with heat. Five minutes later, as I hurry downtown, my lungs no longer burning, I jump at the ping of another text.

Hungry? Dennis asks.

I'm buying, I reply.

Where?

I know a place. I text him the location.

Never heard of it.

Just meet me there.

I promised Dennis a VR experience. It's time to make good.

Not much later we're on the steps of the VR Café. I've grabbed a couple of burritos from the food truck across the road.

"That was crazy." I give him a hard high five.

"That was awesome," Dennis says. "I came to watch. When I walked in, the nurse was pushing through the door and glaring at you, so I ran back to the washroom, shoved all my clothes in my backpack and—"

"I caught the rest. Was that Blackpink?"

"One of their biggest hits." He hums a few bars, and I shake my head.

"Never heard it, but thanks. I'd be in hospital jail if it weren't for you."

"Can you imagine how bad hospital jail food is?"

"I owe you," I say.

Dennis snorts. "You owe me nothing. You gave me your sister."

"What do you mean?" I ask.

He places his hand on my shoulder and stares at me. "Your family could have blocked the organ donation. Her having registered is part of it, but the family can stop the donation. You didn't. That takes courage."

I flush with shame. I did no such thing. I threw myself over her and threatened to stick the endotracheal tube down Dr. Lebow's throat. I was rude to the nurses and angry with my parents for not fighting harder for Minnie.

"It takes so much courage. I can't imagine how you could find that strength in the depths of despair. The worst moment really, right? When everything is against you. You said you wanted to be sure her death helped others." His head swings in wonderment even as the blood drains from mine.

"Well, thanks anyway." I break away, uncomfortable with his words and his familiarity. "Follow me." I head into the café, where I rent a "cell."

"Welcome to the ultimate VR playing arena."

"No way!" Dennis says, scrambling to hold the holy grail of VR gear, a wireless headset. He stands in the middle of a green cell, the playing area. A screen hangs in front of him.

"It's all yours for the entire hour. They have games here that haven't even been released."

"Wow." Dennis slides the headset on, grabs the slim hand controls and selects a zombie game.

"Careful what you wish for, man."

On the screen, Dennis appears in a sewer, gripping an ax. Zombies begin to shamble toward him from different tunnels. He takes a swing and catches a zombie in the torso.

"Watch it. You've got one behind you," I say.

"So did you get what you were after?" The ax arcs, and the zombie head rolls.

"I hope so," I reply and pick up my phone to connect to the café's free Wi-Fi.

"Good, because I don't think you can go back there."

I laugh. "Never." I start swiping through the photos I snapped of the computer screen. A couple are blurry, but the last one—the most important one—isn't. The list of names. My heart sister.

"Rebecca Shih," I say.

"You got a name?" Dennis asks. He lifts the headset. Three zombies are chewing on his avatar.

"Uh, you're losing brains."

"This is so much more important!" He leaves the cell and pulls a laptop from his backpack. "I'll do a search. Shih? Maybe she's single." Dennis waggles his eyebrows.

"No way," I say too quickly. "You can't."

He chuckles. "What? You like her? She's your heart sister. You're not even allowed to date her!"

"That's not what I meant." I don't really know what I mean. It just seems weird to talk like this about someone so connected to my sister. "Besides, then you'd be dating your cousin."

"Second cousin. That's allowed."

"You'd date your—forget it. I don't want to date her. I want to meet her. Get to know her. She's my heart sister."

"Wow," Dennis says, staring down at his screen.

I stand over Dennis's shoulder so I can see. "What?"

Dennis has found her Instagram feed. Except her username isn't Rebecca Shih. It's Dark Heart. All moody purple and silvers. Images of powerful women cut through castle gates with massive burning blades. Women on the backs of dragons slay monstrous nightmares with tentacles, beaks and muscle corded with veins.

"Is that her art?" I ask.

"Yup. She's into heavy metal."

"Holy crap. She's good." Minnie's heart found the right home. "Keep scrolling!"

Dennis sighs when I pull the laptop away from him, and he switches to his phone. Dark Heart hasn't posted in a few weeks. Before then she'd posted almost daily. "Try Twitter," Dennis says. "These are scans of watercolors, but if she posted something from her phone, it might have the geographical data of where it was taken embedded in it."

I search for Dark Heart on Twitter and only find some people reposting her art.

"Uh-oh," Dennis says, holding up his phone screen. "Facebook."

"It's not my first choice of social media, but I won't hold it against her," I say.

"No, the uh-oh part is one of her posts."

I read from his screen. I'm not taking visitors quite yet, okay?

In the comments "Uncle Kain" asks where he can send care packages, and "Becca" Shih responds, The pediatric intensive care unit of Toronto General Hospital.

"Posted yesterday," Dennis says.

"No way." I slump. My heart sister is still in the hospital. The *same* hospital I just hacked. The one to which I can never return.

"If you want to meet her, you'll have to go back." Dennis slips the headset on again and hits *reset*, shouldering the ax.

"But I can't, right? I really can't." I'd rather fight zombies for real.

SIXTEEN

I long to be alone. Leaving Dennis to play, I push out of the VR Café, grimace at the leaking garbage bags on the street corner and make for the subway. I lean my forehead against the cool window of the subway car, listening to the conductor's announcements and thinking about how there's nothing we can do to keep the train from moving. At my station the people disperse, and I stumble home along the quiet of our street.

In the kitchen my mom spoons frost-burned ice cream into her mouth.

"I'll make you something, Mom." The burrito bobs guiltily in my stomach.

"Not hungry, really," she says, holding a pink dripping spoonful.

Every part of her droops. Stringy hair. Eyelids. Lips. Shoulders. But she's up, and that has to be a good sign.

"I can make spaghetti. Maybe a few meatless balls.

Or have something delivered?" My mouth falters in its attempts to grin, lips pulling down instead. "We haven't ordered in for a while."

She sighs and then sighs again. She musters the energy to lift her hand enough to knock the now-empty carton into the sink.

"I may have found the person who received Minnie's heart," I say.

My mom stops and lifts her head.

I go to the sink and start to rinse the carton. "She's artistic too. Like Minnie. Maybe even around the same age. I'm trying to meet her."

Mom starts shaking. It starts with her head and travels down her arms. I shut off the tap and hurry toward her, but she rushes to her bedroom and closes the door. I retreat to my room.

I sit at my desk. How to turn my mother's despair into joy? Even an inch toward joy. I feel like the mouse directing squirrels in Minnie's diorama. *I don't know how to direct this scene.* A good scene takes the character from one emotional pole to the other. I take out a sheet of paper. Rebecca might have answers.

Dear...

I know her name now. So why write letters? I should just sneak into the PICU and find her room. Except she doesn't want to meet me, and if I were caught, I could go to jail. I need a disguise. I can't dress up as a doctor or a nurse again.

My phone bleeps a reminder to call Joey. I shut my eyes. It's too much responsibility. Where is Minnie?

My fingers whiten on the phone. At least my last call with Joey went well. My efforts are helping at least one person.

I dial and reach Joey's voice mail. I call three more times, and on the third Joey answers, "Yeeeah, heeeey." There's an unnatural length to the words.

"How are you keeping, Joey?" I ask.

"Oh, you...know..." Again with the drawn-out vowels. He breathes heavily into the receiver.

"What kept you from drinking today?" It's a limp question, barely asked.

"Weeell, I did pretty good." He chortles.

"Crap, Joey, are you drunk?"

"There's druunk, and theen there's druunk."

I hang up. I'm shaking. I've failed. I bury my face in the crook of my arm. It's going to be a process, I tell myself—but that only makes sense if I know what to do next. On the sheet of paper I write:

Dear Heart Sister,

Tell me more about what you'll do with your new heart. Please? You asked whether I want to be famous. Well, I want to be a movie director, so in some ways I have to be famous to be successful, and I want to be a success. Why a director? Directors shape stories. And a good story makes you think.

What's it like to lose a sister? I can tell you that losing a sister is like living without a heart. I have these stabbing pains where it once was—I didn't know sadness would be so physical. My mom has it the worst, crippling spasms of pain. Mine is more of a hollowness that I sometimes forget about, but when I'm about to look at my sister and find her gone, I remember all over again.

She's my twin. We always had each other. I had never gone more than a day without seeing her, and she knew me better than anyone else in the world. I'm so scared of having to do it alone. I don't want to be alone.

What helps you through everything?

I drop my pen and work to splice the different green-screen videos into the one of Minnie by the campfire. On that summer night when I filmed her, I answered Minnie's questions too. Maybe my pre-death answers hold some solutions. When I could think. Before everything changed.

EXT. CAMPFIRE - NIGHT

Around the campfire, MINNIE (16) sits with EMMITT (16). She has her guitar across her knees and plucks absently at the strings without realizing she's doing it. She grins at him, face aglow, sparks flying into the night.

MINNIE
What's your name?

                    EMMITT
Emmitt.

                    MINNIE
If you were an animal,
what would you be?

Emmitt laughs. Minnie always
makes him laugh. The answer
comes so easy.

                    EMMITT
Mouse wins, right?

                    MINNIE
If I were to put you
in a diorama, what
would it look like?

                    EMMITT
My diorama? I'm the
one who brings people
stories. I bring
people into stories.
Okay, okay, so it's a
film set.

Emmitt holds his hands so that
his fingers frame the shot.

> EMMITT (CONT'D)
> No, we're at the
> Academy Awards. You're
> there for sure. But
> you'd be a seven-headed
> cat. I'm receiving the
> Lifetime Achievement
> Award. This is
> possible, you know it
> is...

Emmitt is right. Anything is
possible. He is lucky, but
he doesn't realize how short-
lived and shallow that dream
will be.

> MINNIE
> Cool. What would other
> people put in your
> diorama?

> EMMITT
> I have a lot to prove.
> Unlike you, certain
> other people don't
> think I can do this.
> They think I should
> be an accountant or a
> bean butcher.

(beat)
I have to believe in
myself. I have a twist
though. I want to be
like Quentin Tarantino
in the virtual-reality
world. I guess I
haven't answered the
question though, have
I? People would see me
in a coffee shop, with
my paws pulling my
hair out. Alone.

MINNIE
How can you make the
diorama better?

EMMITT
Virtual reality, see.
  (leaning forward)
Imagine I'm in the
diorama, onstage at
the Academy Awards,
but I have a headset
on and am in VR at
the same time. It's
so meta. I'm at the
pinnacle of my career
and yet existing

somewhere terrifying
at the same time. Like
a refugee camp. Or in
a bombed-out city.
    (laughing)
See, if we can always
be aware of our luck,
share the viewpoints
of others, we can
save the world. We'll
create empathy, right?
When someone is shot
on the other side of
the world, we shrug.
When it's our neighbor,
we drop everything
to help. That's what
VR can do. It'll make
everyone a neighbor.

Emmitt's eyes sparkle. He
believes this. Minnie grins
back.

              FADE OUT.

I barely recognize myself in the video. My hair is
clean-cut and parted to one side. My skin shines. I have
my mother's broad forehead, and it's smooth and clear of
acne. My smile seems so ready, so careless.

I take off the headset, and a disheveled, zitted, worried Emmitt stares back from the mirror. I pat down a cowlick.

I kneel beside Minnie on the butcher paper. I'll never forget her answers when I asked the same questions of her.

I pick up a red marker. Instead of coloring in Minnie's heart, I draw bigger and bigger outlines of hearts in different colors. The heart I'd drawn before is far too small. Soon a rainbow of hearts fills her chest.

I told my heart sister that Minnie's dioramas made her different from me, but that's not really true. Minnie's dioramas try to capture human truths. Doesn't film do the same?

I bring people into stories. I hold on to that. That's my job, and through it I will bring my family together. But first I need a disguise that will allow unfettered access to the PICU. I snap the caps back on the markers.

It's time to find my inner clown.

SEVENTEEN

Surprise. There's a shortage of volunteer clowns.

When I ask the hospital volunteer coordinator if I can be a clown, she claps her hands together and cries, "Why, yes you can!"

Inside her office, away from security guards, I relax and tug the hoodie from my head. The small room has a side entry into the gift shop, which the volunteers appear to run as well. At a desk a sewing machine is piled with fabric and spools of thread. Several mobile carts line a wall, one cart full of craft supplies, another of books and one of posters of music bands.

The woman comes around her desk and looks ready to hug me, her smile wide. I keep my arms tight to my sides, and she seems to think better of it.

"I'm Fatima. Welcome. Do you have any clowning experience?" I start to shake my head, and she waves off her question and tucks a stray hair back into her violet hijab. "No matter. No experience is necessary. We have everything you need."

"That's good," I say. "Because if you left it to me, I'd probably end up looking like the clown from Stephen King's *It*."

"Oh, we really don't want that, do we? Now, we start all new volunteers at the beginning of the month. You'll have to wait a couple of weeks."

"What?" I say. "I mean, I was really hoping to start sooner."

"Why?"

"School will begin, and I won't be able to come in as often."

Fatima continues, as if second-guessing her initial enthusiasm. "Well, perhaps we can make an exception for the right person. How about juggling? Can you do that? Or magic tricks? The kids love magic tricks. Adults too."

"I can make cookies disappear," I say.

She smiles, grips my shoulders and studies my face. Hers radiates warmth like an open fire. I offer her the best smile I can manage.

"Well, the tricks are easy. Squirting flowers, never-ending handkerchiefs, honking nose—we have them all. But, you know, people really only need some company. Do you like talking to people?"

I nod, painfully aware of how she is doing all the talking. Her face falls. "What brought you here?"

"Oh, uh, I..." I stammer. "Helping people is good?" And I realize I'm about to lose a job I never had that I wouldn't have been paid for and that they desperately need someone to do. "Look, I'll be honest. I need the volunteer hours to graduate."

"We always have a few desperate kids this time of year." She compresses her lips. "So that's what this is all about?"

"Well, yeah, but I *want* to do this too. I'm not graduating this year. I'm into movies. And I do impressions."

She raises an eyebrow. Maybe she's picking up on my ulterior motive.

"Pick a movie," I say.

"*Casablanca.*"

"One that isn't ancient."

She squints at me. "Fine. *Die Hard.*"

"Still ancient, but I can work with that." I give her my best Bruce Willis impression. "'Welcome to the party, pal.'"

"Not bad," she says. "Now try *Terminator.*"

"Easy. 'I need your boots, your clothes and your motorcycle,'" I say in Arnold's signature monotone.

I can tell it's working because her eyes light up again.

"*Breaking Bad.*"

"That's TV," I say in a perfect imitation of Walter White. "My name is Emmitt Highland. I live at 422 Riverdale Avenue, Toronto, Ontario, M4W 2T2. This is my confession. If you're watching this tape, I'm probably dead. Murdered by Fatima for failing to make people laugh."

"Ha! And you're right. I'll kill ya." Her expression hardens for a moment, and then she laughs. "Okay, well, let's try this out. Clown suit is in that cupboard there, and shoes are in the closet."

I grab the massive red shoes. They're designed to slide on over my sneakers. "Big shoes to fill," I say.

"Start with the pediatric ward. Ask the nurses which rooms to hit."

"Oh, I was hoping I could start with the PICU."

She squints at me. "And the reason being...?"

I think fast. "Because they're *really* sick."

"Trust me—most of them wouldn't even know you were there. The kids in the general ward are sick enough."

I'm caught. "You sure? I had a friend in the PICU. She said it was soooo boring."

"They try to limit people on the floor because of infections, with everyone being so immunocompromised. Besides, the last time we sent in a clown, some kid threatened him with a tracheotomy. Our best clown, and he quit."

Oops. I flush. That was me. "Okay, I'll go where you think I'm of best use." I'll figure something out later.

Fatima motions to the open cupboard. I pull on red pantaloons, a bright blue blouse with yellow polka dots, and a black hat. "Very traditional," I say.

Fatima gives me the thumbs-up. "Let me help with your makeup."

She sits me down and first spreads on a white base, then the giant red lips and the black diamond eyes. There's something relaxing about having someone paint my face, despite the waxy taste of the makeup.

When she's done, she takes the red nose, pinches it so it looks like red Pac-Man and slides it over mine. She honks it and laughs. She'd be an amazing clown.

"Almost ready," she says.

My face feels tight from the drying face paint. I spot the puffy rainbow wig she's headed for and sigh. In the mirror a classic clown grins back at me. At least no one will recognize me. Not that there's much risk of that if I'm on the wrong ward.

"When you're done in pediatrics, come on back, and we'll see how the day is going. But first you have to fill out some forms. And I'll be needing your ID."

"My ID?"

"Yes, a driver's license, if you've got it, but I'll take your student card."

I hesitate but have no choice. I dig underneath the costume to my pocket and smile as I hand it to her. I feel like I'm lighting a fuse.

As Fatima studies my school ID, I sign my name on a privacy statement and code of conduct. When I'm done, she hands me a volunteer badge to hang around my neck.

"And, Emmitt, thanks for doing this. Not many kids your age want to spend the day in a clown suit."

Big surprise.

EIGHTEEN

As I leave Fatima's office, I nearly get taken out by a man being whisked past on a gurney. Once it's safe again, I flex my feet, trying to keep the toes of the two-foot-long shoes up so I don't trip. I waddle toward a wall map of the hospital.

"Can I have a sword?" a little girl asks me as I inspect the map. "A balloon sword?" I give her an exaggerated frown and a helpless shrug. She scowls at me and runs away. As I make my way to pediatrics, on the far side of the hospital, I wave at wide-eyed kids and huffing, grumpy old men. The costume—its anonymity—is freeing. It gives me permission to be silly, a little like how Minnie's really loud singing gave me permission to join her at karaoke. By the time I reach the doors to the ward, my entire body moves with each wave, and I'm working on a goofy laugh that annoys even me. I honk my nose at a nurse, who regards me with a hard, humorless stare. I honk again and goofy-laugh.

"And you are?" she asks.

I need a name. "Dr. Happy," I say.

"You can't be doctor anything. It confuses the children." She stares at me hard again.

"Dappy?" I try.

"Dappy the Clown. Great. You can start in the common area," she says. "Where I can keep an eye on you."

"Thank you..." I search for her name tag. "Jeannie." *Meanie is more like it.*

I push through the doors. Jeannie follows, high-fiving another nurse and telling her that I'm the new entertainment.

Inside the doors I spot a giant penguin painted on the wall. It has a big carrot in its flipper. I pretend to pat it, and a little girl giggles. She is towing an IV pole.

"I think this penguin wants to be a rabbit," I say. Then I waddle like a penguin toward the sounds of a television playing. I assume it's the common room. I'll spend a few minutes there and then see if I can figure out a way to penetrate the PICU.

When I enter the room, a kid nearly my age spots me. "You gotta be fuh—"

"Language," Jeannie cautions. I notice that the girl is wrapping a bandanna around her hairless head. She returns to watching the television. A boy of about six or seven scrambles on a kid-friendly sculpture of a penguin surfing across some ice. Not sure what the penguin theme is all about. The walls are painted with happy snow scenes. On the couch slumps a second, younger girl whose expressionless face reminds me of my mom. She shivers under quilts.

"Positive distraction," Jeannie says to me. "I'm watching to be sure you don't terrorize the kids."

"What?"

She grabs me by the shoulder. "That's your job. Positive distraction. Get on with it." Then she pulls out her phone and proceeds to ignore me.

I goofy-laugh, and the older girl turns up the volume on the television. She's bone thin, with hollow cheeks and dark wheels around her eyes, but her posture is amazing—like she has a rod rammed through her back.

"I'm Dappy!" I exclaim, but no one looks at me. Jeannie rolls her eyes. "Maybe I should come back when they're not so tired?" I say to her.

Jeannie squints, and I understand the message. Get on with it.

"What's your name?" I ask the little boy.

"Isaac."

"Do you want to honk my nose?"

It pinches as he squeezes until it honks. He blinks, smiles and honks again. "You could be a professional nose honker when you grow up," I say. He goes back to climbing on the penguin.

I shuffle over to the little girl on the couch. "What's your name?"

Her chin dips beneath her quilt.

"Edith," Jeannie answers for her.

"Well, that's a nice name. My great-aunt was named Edith. She had a lot more wrinkles that you do though."

The girl doesn't laugh.

"Positive…distraction. *Positive*," Jeannie says.

"Well, Edith." I honk my nose, and she shies away. I search my pocket and find a silk handkerchief. But when I pull it out, it keeps coming, so I keep pulling and it keeps streaming from the pocket. I chuckle, not sure myself when the endless-handkerchief trick will end. When it finally does, I glance up to see if Edith's watching. She's not. I stuff the silk back into my pocket, which takes twice as long as it did to pull it out. Jeannie goes back to her phone. Isaac's happy enough on his penguin, which leaves the grumpy teen.

"Hey, Edith," I hiss conspiratorially. "Watch this." I walk over to the teen and take off my wig. I hold it over her head. Edith's eyes widen. I drop the wig over the bandanna. The girl, now wearing a rainbow Afro, slowly stands and walks out of the room. She looks furious. A moment after she disappears through the doorway, the wig flies back into the room and hits the nurse.

"Now I have lice!" The girl's shout echoes down the hall.

I turn to the nurse. "She can't," I say. "I mean, have lice. Not without hair."

"Nice," says the nurse. But I catch Edith grinning for a second before turning back to the television. Of course, Mean Jeannie doesn't notice. She leans in, looks me in the eye and says, "You know, your job here is to bring a little joy to the short time some of these kids might have left."

I flush with sudden shame.

"I'll practice," I say. "Anyone else you want me to… distract? I can try."

"I think that's enough for today," the nurse says and points back the way we came. The penguin is still waving. The clock says it's been ten minutes. As I leave, I hear the television channel change in the common room. I failed them. Their reality sucks, and I did nothing to improve it. *I bring people into stories.*

Sure I do.

NINETEEN

I try to remind myself that my goal had not been to cheer up some sick cancer kids but to infiltrate the defenses of the PICU waiting area and track down Rebecca Shih. My failure in pediatrics could be viewed as success. Still, I can't shake the bandanna girl's anger and the nurse's disappointment. As I enter the dimly lit waiting room in my clown suit, I feel like a penguin wielding a carrot. Out of place and more than a little wrong.

I wave at a row of somber people, their faces ghostly. Only a little old lady wearing a powder blue dress fringed with lace smiles. In the far corner I recognize two members of the family from the other day. They've staked out their territory with a mess of soda cans and chip bags. Fast-food wrappers and coffee cups set the borders of another family in crisis. At the nursing station, the charge nurse purses his lips, eyes following me. I start forward. The more confident I am, the better chance I have of allaying suspicion.

"Hey!" I say. "I'm Dappy the Clown, and I'm here to cheer up the wonderful patients of your unit!"

The nurse's eyebrows arch. "Well, Dappy, that sounds like a great idea, but why don't you work the waiting area. How's that?" He returns to his charts.

"Well, I'd be Dappy to!" I reply, trying to channel the enthusiasm of Dennis. "Laughter is the best medicine— that's what they say!" I grin like a goofball. The nurse's arms cross. I am not winning him over.

"Just do your job, clown," the nurse replies, eyes back on the screen. At least he didn't recognize me. And no Wanted posters are plastered on the wall. I've broken through the first line of defense, but I need to keep moving forward.

Beyond those doors awaits my heart sister. To get in there, I must remain focused on the task at hand. I am about to offer a crying woman the endless handkerchief when I remember what Fatima said. Most of these people only want someone to talk to.

I start with the little old lady who smiled at me earlier, sliding into the vacant seat beside her. At her sweet smile, I relax and return a grin. She shifts closer.

"When's the naked boy coming?" she asks with a wink.

"Naked boy?" I say. "I don't know what you're talking about."

She waggles her eyebrows. *Crap. She totally recognizes me!* I put a finger to my lips.

"It's okay. I won't tell. That was the most fun I've had since I arrived."

"How'd you recognize me?"

"I'm good at eyes."

"What are you in for?" I ask.

"Sixty-seven years," she replies. "Of marriage."

I laugh. "Sounds frightening."

"It was wonderful." The wrinkles around her eyes deepen. "It really was. My darling had a heart attack. He's dying." I look around to ensure I'm in the PICU and not the adult ward. "He's down on the second floor," she adds. "I have a great-niece in here. She's only three years old. She's going to be okay. I come up here to visit her and remember how lucky I am."

"I'm sorry about your husband."

She reaches over and pats my arm. "Thank you, but don't be. Sixty-seven years. We had a good life together and a lot of fun. The morning it happened, he told me he loved me to the stars. I'll see him there soon enough."

I've thought a lot about where Minnie is. Whether she is in some heaven. Maybe she's in this very room, hoping I'll do something stupid so she can laugh. Or maybe she's nowhere. Or everywhere, but not in a form I understand. That's probably it—that we can't fathom what life is after death. Because of the not-knowing part, it's scary and sad. But not if you're ready for it. Then maybe it's kind of exciting.

No one was ready for Minnie to die.

I can't stop swallowing. My eyes water. I pull out the handkerchief and dab them.

"Why are you here?" she asks.

"You'll keep a secret?"

"I have so far."

"My sister died here and donated her organs."

"I'm sorry."

"I want to meet the person who received her heart, but I need to disguise myself."

"Because…?" She glances at the nursing station and the scene of the crime.

"Yeah. That."

"Do you think it will help? Meeting her?"

"Oh, it's not for me," I say.

"Hmm. Hmm," she replies.

"Well, maybe a little for me, but I *need* to do this for my mom. I want to film my heart sister and then show my mom. She's having a tough time, right? And I—"

"You were close?"

"My twin."

"Oh, honey," she says and places her hand on mine.

The tears come, and I struggle to dam them with the silk.

The woman chuckles at the pile of handkerchief in my lap. "Uh-oh, now you've done it. You'd better go," she whispers and points at my eyes. "You rubbed away your face paint."

"What?"

"Your face paint. I can see you."

White paint smears the silk handkerchief. I forgot about my makeup. I tuck my chin to my chest, yank the rainbow hair down over my brow and sneak a look at the station. The nurse is still busy with his charts. But then I spot Dr. Lebow coming through the doors. I need to get out of here. I'll try again tomorrow. "Thank you," I say to the woman. "And good luck." I stride out of the waiting area. *Good luck?* To a woman losing her partner of sixty-seven years? What else could I say? How can I cheer up cancer kids? What does anything mean coming from me? Me, who's never had a relationship much longer than sixty-seven days, let alone years?

I hustle back to Fatima. She smiles when she sees me.

"That bad, huh?" she asks. "No one's chasing you, are they?"

I press my face against the frosted glass door, then realize she is joking. "No, no," I say, straightening.

She takes in the smeared face paint. "It's not easy, but it's important. I can mark you down for an hour. Thanks for trying."

She thinks I've been crying about the kids in pediatrics. "I'll be back," I say.

"Really?"

"Sure. I just need to practice. I'll do better. I promise."

Her smile returns. "Well, next time take some balloons. Props can help." She piles several thin multicolored balloons and a balloon pump into my hand. "Practice at home."

"Great, great. Yeah, I'll see you tomorrow."

"Don't make me call security," she adds.

With the door half-open, I freeze. Has my plan been revealed?

"The outfit," says Fatima. "I can't let you leave with it. Remember? I'll kill ya."

TWENTY

On my computer screen a woman stands sheathed in inflated balloons. They wrap around her ankles, shins and thighs. An inflatable duck circles her waist, and her arms are studded with a rainbow of balloon snakes. An octopus strangles her, and on her head is a crown sprouting four eye-topped antennae. With every movement of her twisting hands, her body squeaks. The balloon she works in her hands squirms this way and that. The screen joggles with the amateur camerawork.

I've tried pausing Balloon Mama's YouTube tutorial *Five No-Fail Balloon Animals for the Every-Clown* after every wring of her balloon. The burst carcasses of my failures litter my bedroom floor.

"So just...like...this...and that..." *Squidgy-squeak-squidgy.* "Voilà!" She doesn't really make it look easy. And it's not. She has crafted a perfect giraffe. I cry out as mine explodes. Again. I want to wring her neck.

After my tenth attempt, needing a dose of optimism, I check Mothman's Instagram to see the #goodday posts that I've missed.

Ugly-nest caterpillar moth. Although there's no such thing as an ugly moth. #goodday. A picture of a vomit-colored moth sits above the caption. It actually is kind of ugly, but seeing the beauty is Gerry's gift, not mine. I sure can't see it in my tortured balloons.

Gerry's second post confuses me. **One week to live. #goodday.** It's of a luna moth—like a green manta ray with orange-feathered antennae. It's gorgeous, and I'm stunned that something so beautiful can be found in the city's gardens. But why one week to live? After a quick search, I decipher Gerry's caption. The luna moth lives for only one week. It has no mouth with which to eat. It lives just long enough to mate. I'm relieved that Gerry is okay.

My dad gets home and leans into the doorway of my bedroom. His shoulders slouch, and his eyes are dull. "What's that supposed to be?" he asks, pointing to a balloon animal on my desk. It's the first to survive.

"A cow," I say.

"The intestines of a cow?"

Now that he mentions it, the twisted worms of the balloon do look like intestines. "I'm working on my technique."

"Why are you making animal intestines out of balloons?"

"I don't know, Dad. Why do you make sausages out of vegetables? Why did Minnie make carcasses seem like humans?"

He pauses at the edge in my voice. I start pumping up a new balloon. Hard and fast strokes. What I want to say is, *I'm trying to entertain people in the same waiting room you couldn't step into while waiting to see if your daughter would live or die. Where you couldn't hold your wife, who has only been able to move from her bed to the couch for almost two months.*

The tight mouth of the balloon slips off the pump nozzle and shoots up to the ceiling before fizzing back to the floor. I try again with another red balloon. I pump it, tie it and am soon frustrated by the grating squeaks of each twist, by the ever-present knowledge that it's about to burst and by the way my dad stands silent there. Sometimes I feel like I'm the only one trying.

"What food looks like changes its taste, our enjoyment of it," he replies. "That's why I do it."

"And Minnie?" I ask, surprised at the question bubbling out of me. "Why did she make art out of dead things?"

"Your sister—"

"Minnie," I challenge.

"Your sister, Emmitt, I think she created her art for a number of reasons. I think it connected her to the natural world. Perhaps for her it was a way of illustrating how all living creatures are equal."

That sounds like a radical vegetarian's interpretation.

"Say her name, Dad," I say. "You need to." He swallows and looks past me, over my shoulder. "Her name was Minnie," I continue. "She is dead. I love her.

You love her. We all do. I don't want to erase her by not talking about her."

My dad gives this strangled cough and then says in a whisper, "Not erasing her. No. I'm holding her." He wraps his arms around his chest. "I'm holding on to her, and I can't look right at her. If I do, the illusion breaks. She's right there, in the periphery." His trembling finger points off to the side.

I get it. If he faces her, he'll see that she's gone. That it happened, and she's dead.

His face twists with pain.

"Dad, it's okay," I say, motioning for him to stop, wrestling to hold back the competing emotions of sadness, anger and shame.

"No, you're right. We should talk. I'm sorry." It's as though every one of his muscles flexes. His jaw's bulging. A vein at his temple protrudes thick and purple. His body is clutched by his arms, and his eyes blink quickly as the tears fall. "You need me to talk about her, so I will."

"You've just been so distant."

"Yeah, you're right about that too," he says hoarsely. It hurts, seeing his pain.

He faces me. He sees me. "I don't know how to be anymore, son. All I know is I sure as hell didn't protect her. And that's my *one* job. What am I if I can't do that?" His sad eyes seem to take in the boxes and bare walls of my room as if for the first time.

He roots something out of his pocket and puts it on the desk beside the deformed cow. Something round.

It takes me a moment to realize it's a rutabaga. Carved into a miniature world. An outer layer of trees, then suburbs and a city of skyscrapers beyond. In the middle is a square full of little kids, overlooked by a great tower. A waterfall pours from the tower's top. The rutabaga city is beautiful, but it's already beginning to molder and rot. It's the size of a heart.

"How long have you been working on this?"

"This is my world," he says. My watch alarm bleeps. He draws another breath before asking, "What's that for?"

"A reminder to call a friend. But first…" I pump up a six-foot skinny balloon and then start twisting and twisting. By the time I'm done, it is not clearly a giraffe, but at least I have a multi-legged creature with a pole for a head. I set it beside my dad's rutabaga world and pat him on the shoulder. "I think I should stick to film, Dad, and you should stick to making beautiful edible feasts."

He laughs and then steps in and gathers me into a hug. We're the same height, but his arms hold me powerfully. I swallow hard, and he rushes off, leaving me in my bedroom with his rotting world. After a minute I call Joey.

"Hell…o." Joey's answer is tired and done in—maybe hungover.

I pause to gather myself. It's like the world has sprung leaks, and I only have so many fingers with which to plug the wounds.

"Hi, Liver Brother, it's Emmitt."

A sigh on the other end. I want to get angry, to lay into him. Tell him off for drinking. Instead I start into the questions, "All right, so why—"

"My kids. My kids. A drink won't help. Okay?"

Argumentative, grumpy, but at least he doesn't sound like he's been drinking. That's good. I lean forward.

"You planning to drink tonight?"

"You have the answers to your questions. That's what I owe you, right?"

Remember what Jeannie said. *Positive distraction.*

I glance to the rotting world and balloon intestines.

"Can I tell you about my day?" I ask.

"Be my guest."

I can tell by his tone that he's not really interested. But I tell him about the hospital, why I went there and my failed clowning. By the end I extract a snort of what I hope is laughter.

"So you're not the best clown," he says.

"Understatement of the year."

There's a pregnant pause and then, "Why do you want to meet this heart sister so much? I mean, she's not really your sister. And she clearly doesn't want to talk to you."

I pick up the rutabaga and give it a shake. "She's not my sister. She's my heart sister." How do I explain the connection I feel? "Maybe if my sister had had a kid, I'd love it like I do my heart sister. In a way, she's something that Minnie gave birth to."

"You think your sister gave birth to me?" Joey says.

"Sort of, I guess," I say. "I mean, would you be here otherwise?"

"I'd be more yellow."

"Yeah, so you owe her your pinkish health."

"I'm actually kind of pasty."

"Let's work on that."

"Truth is…" Joey hesitates. "The truth is, I'd probably be dead." His voice gets quieter. "Okay, man. Thanks for today. Now I gotta run." He hangs up before I have a chance to say good night.

Limp balloons strew the desk. Balloons that, with the right skills, could become swords, lions, dragons and pirate ships. Creation is a form of giving birth. I run a finger around the hard plastic of my VR headset. My dad has his world. I have mine. The patients have theirs, but they need distractions from the tough parts.

I grin, an idea taking shape. *I think I should stick to film, Dad.*

"Positive distraction," I whisper. I gather several of my tripods, unscrew the VR system's mounted location-tracking detectors from the wall and pack everything into my bag, along with the leftover balloons and pump. When the bag is packed, I sit down and write to my heart sister.

Dear Heart Sister,

I'm facing some big challenges. It's not about my sister. I'm just sucking. What do you suck at? My sister was great at art and crafts and helping people. I can't think of much she wasn't good at. Maybe that's just how I want to remember her though. It's disturbing.

Sometimes it's hard to remember her. I know everything about my sister, but don't have anything specific to tell unless you ask.

Say you ask me where she got all her creatures to taxidermize. I'd tell you about the urgency in her voice when she spotted a furry lump on the road. Really, you'd think it was a live cat—she'd go rigid with fear. "Emmitt! There!" I've had to stop her from throwing herself into traffic before. She's the only person I know who eagerly opened commercial rat traps, the sort you see at the rear doors of restaurants. Our freezer is out of a horror movie—for rodents anyway. Maybe it's time I empty it.

Write back.

Your Heart Brother

The next morning I go to stuff the note into an envelope and stop. This whole letter-writing thing is ridiculous. This is the twenty-first century! I don't want to wait weeks or days for a reply.

I search my call history for the National Transplant Organization and punch in the number. I'm in luck. Martha answers the phone.

"Hi, Martha. You called me a week or so ago about sending mail to my heart sister. I was wondering, could my heart sister and I correspond with each other anonymously through texting or email?"

"Of course. But it's email only."

"Okay, great. So how would that work?"

"You send me the email, and I'll review it before forwarding it. If the recipient chooses to respond, I'll forward on the content of their email only, without the original email address. Everything will pass through me, and I reserve the right to edit out personal information. Give me twenty-four hours, except on weekends, when I'll need seventy-two hours."

Martha gives me her email address. This process should be faster, but somehow it feels even more censored now that I know the name of the person doing the censoring. I key in the letter to my heart sister and send it to our chaperone. She responds with a smile emoji. And a note: **Your sister was very special!** It's a good thing she can't see my eyes rolling.

TWENTY-ONE

Dressed in my full clown regalia, messenger bag over my shoulder, I approach Jeannie.

"Where do you think you're going?" she asks.

"Dappy reporting for duty, ma'am." I grin. "No one's leaving here negatively distracted."

She smiles, evidently catching my joke, and then her disappointed face returns. "This isn't baseball."

"How's that?"

"You don't get three strikes."

"Oh," I say. "How about two strikes?"

Her gaze travels to my bag. "I'll have to approve anything you plan."

"Of course," I say, *because I need a chaperone for everything.*

"Last chance, Dappy."

The doors swing wide. I wave at the penguin and stride as confidently as one can in giant red shoes. The slaps of the soles echo down the hall.

"Who wants to go to a different world?" I ask the common room. I know how I can positively distract kids in a hospital. I can take them on a field trip. A virtual one.

Isaac, wearing a blue hospital gown, is drawing a dragon with crayons at a table. A teenage boy I haven't met is in a wheelchair close to the table. One of his legs is in a cast, and his torso is in a metal frame. A black halo brace encircles his head.

"Where's Grumpy Girl?" I ask the nurse. She shoots me a look. "The girl with the…" I pat my head.

The girl sits up from the couch. "Grumpy Girl is right here." She pulls the blue kerchief off her head to reveal the scalp beneath. "The bald girl with the cancer."

"Oh, didn't see you there," I say, practicing my goofy laugh again.

"Clearly."

"Sorry."

The new boy's eyes flicker in my direction, his body twitching. Grumpy Girl slumps back down to watch cartoons. Isaac keeps drawing.

I drag my bag over the seamless floor to the television, pull out my laptop, plug it into an electrical socket and then into the back of the television. The television screen goes black.

"You're kidding me," Grumpy Girl says from the couch.

"Just wait," I say. "Jeannie, can I have access to the Wi-Fi?"

She shrugs and hands me a card with the network name and password.

Music blares through the headphones as the system boots. Grumpy Girl's eyes narrow. "What's your name?" I ask the boy with the spinal injury.

"Luke," he says.

"Do you want to drive a race car, Luke?"

"Oh yeah," he says.

"Or you could shoot some aliens or lay siege to a castle." I point at the laptop screen. My account has dozens of game options. "Cook, dance, raid a tomb, go scuba diving, paint, visit the International Space Station—"

"Serve me up some aliens!" Luke says.

"Video games?" Jeannie looks uncertain.

"Better than video games," I reply.

"Virtual reality," Luke explains, leaning forward enough that I worry he'll fall out of the chair. "I've tried it a few times. You know what? I want to drive the race car instead."

"Indy 500, coming up."

Grumpy Girl is giving me her best I-don't-care glare, but she watches as I pry apart the VR headset to jury-rig it for Luke's halo. "Guess we can't take this off, huh?"

"Not if he wants to heal," Jeannie says.

I manage to fit Luke on the headset's loosest setting.

I press the hand controllers into his palm, and his fingers close loosely over them.

"Got it?" I ask.

He nods. Even so, I'm not sure this will work. Jeannie has been watching my every move, eyes unblinking, lips pursed. I probably shouldn't have started with the guy with mobility issues. But here goes nothing. I help Luke with a couple of menu selections and then back off.

On the screen the game starts. Luke's mouth forms an O and then stretches into a grin. Knowing what he's seeing and having played the game before, I give simple directions like "Lift your arm to move the cursor to choose the car" and "Squeeze the trigger to select your option." We are seeing a two-dimensional image on the television screen, but Luke is seeing the world in 3-D. He chooses a sleek-looking Ferrari with a massive engine. I would have upgraded the tires. He then selects the hardest race course—the Devil's Pitchfork.

"A bit confident there, Luke," I say. "Maybe try something easier?"

His jaw clenches. "I got this."

A light does the count—red, yellow, green. Luke's race begins. The competing cars rip past him off the start. Engines roar and tires screech, but Luke's car is left rumbling slowly over the start line.

"Squeeze the right trigger for gas. Go, go!" I call.

Isaac cries, "Go!"

Even Grumpy Girl's hands clench.

The car stutters forward down the course, lurching until finally the throttle sticks, opening wide.

"You'll want to use the brakes going into the turns," I warn.

Luke's having none of it. The engine runs hot.

"Okay, steer, steer," I say as calmly as I can.

The rear spoiler of a competitor rushes toward us as Luke catches the stragglers. His car flies over the rumble strip and off course, kicking up grass, and then fishtails back onto the track. Tires smoke as they bite into pavement again. Luke's arms quake as he lifts the controllers a few inches off the wheelchair arm and jerks them left and right to steer. He's managed to use his pinky to pinch the trigger.

"The next is a tight right turn," I say. "The course is shaped like a pitchfork, and it's the tip on the first tine."

Sweat flows freely down Luke's cheeks. I gasp as he manages the hairpin, sliding past two cars in the process.

"Turn, turn!" I yell. But it's too late.

On the screen the car slams into the wall, flips into the air, smashes back onto the track and rolls before bursting into flames.

"Very realistic," says Jeannie.

"Hey, that wasn't bad for your first time," I tell Luke as I help him remove the headset. I can't tell if he enjoyed himself or not. It's disappointing.

As the nurse leans down to sanitize the headset, she whispers, "Luke's physiotherapist hasn't been able to get him to do that much exercise in a day." And then she winks. "You have my permission to continue."

"Can I go next?" It's Isaac.

I freeze for a moment, stunned. It is one thing to believe the unreal can change reality. It is another to see it.

Encouraged and remembering my getup, I honk my nose. "Sure, Isaac. What'll it be? Race car? Aliens from space?"

"Where else are aliens from?" Grumpy Girl asks.

"Can I draw?" Isaac holds up a crayon.

"You're already doing some pretty awesome drawing right there. You sure you don't want to try something else with this thing?" I mimic firing a laser gun.

He shakes his head. "Nope, drawing."

I haven't actually used the painting application. It seems a bit boring to me. Nothing explodes and there are no quests, but I set Isaac up in front of the screen. "Okay, so you have some space on either side of you and a bit in the front and back. But be careful, or you might end up in Grumpy's lap."

"Okay," says Isaac.

"It's Joy," says the grumpy girl.

"What?"

"My name's not Grumpy. It's Joy."

I laugh. "Of course it is." I turn. "Careful, Isaac, or you might fall on Joy," I say.

Isaac giggles. He takes a practice swing with his paint brush, but the canvas isn't loaded yet.

But then a brush pops up on the screen, along with a series of palette options—paint with smoke, light, fire, rainbow, stars and so on.

"Whoa," he says.

I glance back to see what Isaac had been drawing earlier—a red dragon that's more teeth than anything else. Isaac starts slowly, figuring out the palette system and types of brush options. He's smart and calculating. Most kids his age would have just started scribbling, if only to see what happens. But Isaac is very deliberate. Finally he takes a stroke. The line that appears on the screen is lit like a Jedi's lightsaber.

"Oh yeah," he says.

"Cool," Jeannie says, taking a step forward. Joy sits up. Another slash, and it's a burning *X*.

He steps forward and *through* the painting. "I'm in it! I'm in the painting!" Isaac's passion is infectious as he turns and tangles himself in the cords dangling from the headset.

Isaac clears the canvas, chooses a thinner brush and starts again in earnest. He rushes back and forth. A dozen or so wild creatures soon prowl around the canvas. They all have their mouths open, like they're chasing him.

Is this what's playing inside Isaac's head? Seems more like a nightmare. "You need a knight or something, Isaac, something to fight back with. Give him a giant sword."

Then the kid does something I don't expect. He picks a flaming silver paint, and in the center he draws a tiny stick boy. Into the boy's hand he places not a sword but a series of golden leashes. Like strings holding a bouquet of balloons, the dozen magic cords he grips are all attached to the necks of the creatures. They aren't attacking after all—they're chained to him, enraged by their capture. When he's done, Isaac pulls off the headset and grins. "See, it's me against cancer," he says. "Isaac wins."

Jeannie gasps as he hands the headset to her. She gives him a hug. Then I notice a dragon in the far corner of the scene. Unshackled.

"You forgot a leash," I say.

"No," says Isaac, his smile fading. "That's Edith's dragon. The one that got her while she was sleeping."

I'm speechless. Jeannie shakes her head sadly. I'd forgotten about Edith.

When I glance back to see if Joy's interested in taking a turn, she's gone. Slippered feet pad down the hall. Maybe it all got a little too real.

"Can I try again tomorrow?" I ask the nurse.

"That'd make me so dappy," she says. Ha. So Jeannie can be funny!

"Anything you think Joy would like?"

Jeannie hesitates for a second. "Puzzles."

Which somehow makes perfect sense.

TWENTY-TWO

I shuffle from foot to foot in the hall next to the entrance of the PICU waiting area. With my phone camera, I check my makeup—it's fine. *I can't believe I just checked my makeup.* I draw a deep breath and enter.

The old lady's seat is vacant, which is both a relief and depressing. In their corners, families read and chatter. A man chuckles. Trauma brings some families together, but not mine. Maybe when it's time. When you've had your sixty-seven years of marriage, the kids and grandkids gather and have a party. A "celebration of life." It's a morbid holiday, where the gift is release from pain and a rekindling of family. But tears soaked our kindling, or maybe we're all tending our own fires.

Mine had raged until the end. Hours after they rolled Minnie out to the elevator—Mom trailing with *I love you! We miss you! I'm so proud of you!*—they rolled her back in. Clean. Silent. Unmoving. And long gone. Only then, faced with her corpse and holding a clammy hand, did I turn and leave for home.

The charge nurse waves me in. I hesitate, trying to interpret the curious expression on his face. No one boxes in my exit, though, so I slowly approach. I force my clenched hands to relax.

"Okay, Dappy," the nurse says. "Let's give this a shot."

I'm in? A cold flush rolls over me. "Really?"

"You're here to cheer up the patients, right?" he asks.

"Yeah, yeah, I just—" I'm terrified of meeting my heart sister. I can't have another Joey or, worse, an Eileen. With the letters my heart sister has written, my imagination has turned her into this minor celebrity who can never measure up now. What if she's a racist, homophobic alcoholic? It would send my mother spiraling.

"Well? We heard what you did in pediatrics," he says. "So let's give it a try here."

I give him a white-gloved thumbs-up, and he gestures to the double doors.

I swallow and start to ease forward, hoping to enter quietly and keep a low profile despite the clown costume. But the nurse hits the automatic door opener, which grinds loudly as both doors swing wide open, presenting me to everyone in the hall.

No penguin waves. No gentle music plays. Staff hustle from room to room. Bathed in cool, throbbing light, I suck in the dry, sterile air. To my left a door opens into a patient room. It's room 212—the code blue.

The patient, a super-scrawny boy, is either sleeping or comatose. Nose prongs protrude from his nostrils. I wave just in case he's not unconscious and then continue down the hall.

On this ward, it is all noises—whirring, beeps and the whoosh of ventilators. A tube juts from the mouth of another patient. It reminds me of my sister, but then her eyes blink. The girl's eyes. My sister's eyes never blinked. I shuffle closer.

"Hold on." A tall, gangly nurse runs toward me with hand sanitizer. "No gloves. Certain rooms are masks only, and don't go into room 216 at all. We had a recent *C. difficile* outbreak so are taking extra precautions."

I pull off my gloves and coat my hands in sanitizer. A lemony scent wafts into the air. "Okay, sure." Now I'm second-guessing this whole plan. Why not wait until Rebecca's out of the hospital, when I won't be risking anyone's life?

The nurse considers me for a moment and shakes her head. "Rooms 214, 218, 223 and 226 only. Do you need a television screen for that to work?" She points at my gear.

"No. It's a nice add-on, but a screen is only so more people can watch," I say. "Makes it more social."

"Two fourteen," she repeats. I start in, but she stops me. "That's 213. He's…well, he's not a candidate for clowning. That one." She points.

It's a room down. I can only hope that one of the four rooms I'm allowed in is Rebecca's. This is a start, at least. A chance to scout.

I knock on the door frame. A young dude with prongs in his nostrils and over-ear headphones pulled over white hair nods rhythmically to a really slow beat. All those tubes are not great for VR headsets, but I suppose if I can manage a spinal halo, I can handle a few tubes. His eyes are heavily lidded, skin ashen, and his head moves like an oil rig pumping oil despite him looking about my age or a year older.

"Hiya," I say.

On the blanket, wrist harpooned by an IV line, his hand lifts a fraction. "I can hear." And I realize his head nods aren't in sync with music but rather his breathing.

I continue. "I'm asking around, seeing if anyone wants to try a VR game."

"Yeah, yeah sure." His voice rasps, the well running dry. He pushes down on the bed with his palms as if to sit up but doesn't really go anywhere.

I can see why the nurse asked about the television. His is set high in the corner and would be difficult for me to plug into. Coming into the room, I am doused in the reek of urine. I unzip my bag.

"Any particular type of game you like?" I ask.

"To be honest…" He takes a break. "I'd like to blow…some stuff away."

I smile, and he looks back sadly, focused on breathing.

"You have full use of your arms and hands?"

He lifts his arms. They move slowly, as if passing through water, and wave like kelp stalks, fingers wriggling, tubes trailing. Tattoos rope up his arms.

"Nice tats," I say.

"You have…any…?"

"Ink?" I swallow. "Nah, my parents won't let me." The tattoo on my shoulder burns as hot as my cheeks. "All right, let's take out some alien nasties."

"I hate alien nasties," he replies and chokes on his own laughter. When he's done coughing, I hold up the headset.

"You ready?"

"What's your name?" he asks, pulling off his headphones and setting them beside him.

I had to give Fatima my real ID, but I can't use my real name here. "Emerson," I say. I have to pray no one talks to each other. It feels like I've started a ticking clock. It's only a matter of time before I'm caught in one of my lies or someone starts connecting the dots.

"Emerson, I'm Tom. I have renal failure. Sorry about the smell. It's because stuff builds…in me that my kidneys can't…process."

"Didn't notice," I say.

"Then you need a nose transplant…as much as I need a kidney." More choking laughter. "My mom and sisters will be in later." I think he's telling me that he's not alone, as if he knows I'm here to fill people's time. But loneliness is a wound as real and festering as any other.

"They can try it too, if I'm still around."

"Or I'm still around." He laughs. I don't. "Sorry," he adds. "It's just that more people die on the kidney list than any of the others."

"What do you miss most?" I ask. "Being in here."

"Hanging with friends," he replies. "And video games." He smiles.

For a second I think maybe Tom should have had Minnie's kidney instead of Eileen. But it's impossible to know if that was even an option. Maybe he had the wrong blood type. Maybe he wasn't on the list yet, or the kidney was the wrong size. I may not like Eileen's values, but I can't make those sorts of choices either.

Tom takes the headset and slips it over his eyes. His hands scrabble at the air for the controllers. "Watch out for the multi-legged aliens. They come from behind," I say as I secure the loops over his wrists in case he drops the controllers.

I catch the sounds of him gearing up—weapons, armor, profile choices. Each one chunks heavily through the headphones. The two-dimensional version of his playing field shows on my laptop, but it's not the same thing as being in it—not even close. Tom flubs around. It's the same for everyone new to virtual reality. It takes a while to adjust to the controllers and the environment. The controllers are relatively simple. Two triggers. The thumb uses a trackpad to select different weapons and shields. He's learning, but at this rate I won't have time to hit all the rooms I'm allowed to visit.

I have to be back home soon if I'm going to call Joey, start dinner for my mom, ventilate my family. At best I can share one more VR experience before leaving. I decide to investigate the other rooms while Tom plays, so I can be sure to hit Rebecca's next. "I'll be back in a few minutes," I tell him.

Lost in the game, Tom doesn't respond.

Outside the room, I sip relatively cleansing breaths of the hospital's filtered atmosphere. *Keep moving.* I walk casually by each doorway, peeking in as I pass by.

The staff hardly gives me a second glance, despite my colorful uniform. I spot Dr. Lebow and duck into 218. The room farthest from the nursing station. The one on which I called the code. I tuck into the door frame, and Dr. Lebow strides past.

"I understand," a voice whispers. "They keep poking me too."

I glance up and flush. "Sorry," I say. "Just playing hide and..."

Black hair fans out on her pillow. She scratches at blotchy skin with black painted fingernails. Red bloodshot eyes peer as if through a fog. I've seen corpses on newscasts that look healthier. Her bloated cheeks and body seem like those of a drowning victim.

"Hide and hide?" the girl finishes for me.

"Can I help you?" A man at her bedside folds a magazine, the one from the waiting room.

"Ebola fighters," I say, scrambling to make conversation. "*Time* magazine's Person of the Year 2014. That's a...good one."

The man shows the girl the magazine. I was right.

"What is he, some kind of clown savant?" the girl asks the man.

"No, no, I'm sorry, I was—" I stop. Pinned to a corkboard on the wall with several *Congratulations!* cards are my letters. Around them are drawings—drawings and paintings signed by Dark Heart. My eyes dart to the girl in the bed and back to the board, heat rushing through me. It's Rebecca. Becca. I try to cover my surprise by studying the art.

"Wow," I say. A heavily armored woman riding a fusion of dragon and lion. Despite her musculature, she battles an impossibly large foe, the entire background consumed by the beast's chest, the woman's jagged sword burning through its sternum. There's a charcoal sketch of the same woman climbing a cliff, and another has her gripping the mast of a ship tossing in the sea. A half-finished doodle shows her sleeping, tucked into the flank of her dragon. Brought together by their shared wounds. "These are incredible."

"Thanks," she says. "Who are you?"

Suddenly I remember that Becca told me in one of her letters how important trust is to her. And I'm a clown spy.

"Umm. I don't know."

"Are you okay?" she asks.

"Yeah." I run a hand through my rainbow curls. "I... um...have a virtual-reality headset." I point at the open door. "I'm supposed to show it to you."

"I've tried them before," she says and then clears her throat. "Sorry, they finally removed the breathing tube. Still getting used to speaking again. Forget the cracking of my chest—the breathing tube was the worst."

"Oh, sorry?" Now that I'm here, I have nothing to say. She's less excited about virtual reality than I would have hoped.

She shrugs and chuckles. "No, no, don't be. Not too long ago, I was mostly dead."

I cringe. Now she's not dead. But Minnie is. Rebecca's expression sours. "It's not pretty, I know," she adds. "I'm still reanimating. I think they actually waited until I was fully dead before deciding to find me a heart."

"Ouch, that's blunt."

"You *are* a funny clown," she says.

The man snorts. "Virtual reality, you were saying?"

"Oh, yes." My head's about to burst. "The nurse thought you might like the positive distraction."

Another of her laughs rings out. Among the bleeps and pumps it's a rare, fragile thing. She shrugs. "Sure, why not."

When one of her monitors gives another bleep, I realize it's her heart-rate monitor. It's my sister's heart beating. Right here. Eighty-four beats per minute.

"Okay," I say. "I have to go get the gear."

I head for the door and then pause. "What's your name?"

"Rebecca," she replies. "Becca."

"I'll be right back, Becca."

"And *I* will stay right here." She laughs again.

I turn and stride as fast as I can down the hall.

"Hey," someone calls.

I keep moving.

"Wait up, clown." Dr. Lebow points at me from where the hall turns the corner. "I need to talk to you."

I'm caught. She stares at me as she strides down the hallway.

"You're the kid with the VR system, right?" she asks when she's closer. I swallow, tense, ready to bolt.

"Yeah."

"I've heard it's very popular with the patients. I've always wanted to try it. Can you come set it up in the staff room?"

"But there is another patient who—" I start.

"I only have a few minutes to spare." She points into the room marked *Staff Only*.

I bite back my anger and remind myself how far I've come. I'm *so* close. "Okay, Doctor. Give me a minute."

TWENTY-THREE

Dr. Lebow follows me into Tom's room. "Time's up, Tom."

"More gallows humor. Thanks, Doc," Tom replies, both hand controllers pointing at the doctor as he pulls the triggers. "You were right. The multi-legged ones totally get me."

"I have no idea what you're talking about," Dr. Lebow replies. "Sounds like a nightmare."

"He's talking about the aliens," I say.

"Oh, I see."

"If you listen hard, you can hear them coming—all those feet." Tom eases off the headset, his cheeks ruddier than I recall. "Thanks...what's your name again?"

"Uh..." I glance up at the stained ceiling tiles.

Dr. Lebow laughs. "These trick questions, always tripping up you kids."

"Dappy," I reply.

"Real. Name." Lebow's grin slowly withers as she

regards me. The fake name I gave Tom is stupidly close to my real one.

"Emerson."

"Well, Emerson, let's go." Dr. Lebow carries the headset out, and I need to keep up or pull the cords from the laptop.

"Hey, Doc," Tom calls behind us. "Find me that kidney, okay?"

Dr. Lebow offers him a thumbs-up. I grit my teeth.

When we enter the staff room, I keep my head lowered. Several other people are in here. They've cleared a ten-by-ten area in the center for the perimeter setup. A TV screen is positioned on a table off to the side, and chairs are stacked in a corner. A coffee maker spits coffee as it brews a pot. Beside it a doctor grips a cup of coffee and stares off at the floor. He's pale and haggard, but it's the haunted eyes I notice.

"Success?" Dr. Lebow asks him. He slowly nods, eyes flicking to the status of the coffee maker. "Recovery in Thunder Bay, right?"

"Twelve hours total. Wish it had been a fit for 212 though. He's a DNR now."

"Such a shame."

I focus on the job, plugging in the gear and ensuring the connection to the television screen.

"What reality will I be entering, Emerson?" Dr. Lebow asks.

I squint at the options, annoyed that she's keeping me from my heart sister. "Cooking?" I suggest.

"No, no, I want to do something I've never done before."

I decide on a travel experience. Impressive but hopefully not too time-consuming. "How about a trip to Mount Everest?"

In the middle of the open space, Dr. Lebow has her hand controllers stretched out, and she slowly shuffles in a careful circle, as if concerned with her footing. On the screen, she gazes from Everest's peak.

"Amazing," she murmurs. "Absolutely amazing."

At the chink of an ice hammer, she turns. A heavily loaded Sherpa climbs into view, grinning, goatee frosted like my morning Mini-Wheats.

Dr. Lebow already has a handle on the controllers. Suddenly she's flicking through the travel library, and then she enters a Borneo jungle at night. The jungle floor sparkles, lit by thousands of pinpricks of light. She bends to inspect the pretty lights and jumps right back up again—a blanket of spiders surrounds her. Several people cry out. She giggles. Actually *giggles*.

"Not on your life," Dr. Lebow says, brushing one hand controller across her shoulder.

The screen flashes, and now she is paddling a canoe on a river safari—a broad sweep of the Zambezi stretches before the bow. Nearby half a canoe lies overturned on the bank. Paddles splash. Muddy water brushes near the gunwales of the gear-laden canoes. A hippo spots her entering his harem's territory. The mottled purple hide submerges like a submarine, moving more and more rapidly toward its target. A wake of water speeds toward the canoe as the paddler takes frantic strokes. A nurse calls, "Hippeedo!" and everyone laughs.

Dr. Lebow is serious about canoeing. She glances back once as the canoe moves on. The hippo surfaces where the canoe had been.

Finally the doctor nudges the headset up. "Thank you," she says, with a sincerity that causes me to blush beneath my makeup.

"That's the most vacation time you've taken in a year," someone jokes.

Dr. Lebow hands the headset to someone I recognize. It takes me a moment. The orderly who used to change Minnie's sheets.

"You have anything more actiony, Emmitt?" he asks.

Emmitt. He called me Emmitt. I fumble the game options, dropping a hand controller. As I bend down to retrieve it, I use my free hand to keep the wig in place, trying to hide my panic.

"It's Emerson," Dr. Lebow says.

"Sorry. Anything with a bit more action to it, Emerson?" From the floor, I switch the experience to a first-person shooter game. "That'll do."

Sweat trickles down my back. No one appears to have caught the orderly's slip, but the longer I spend in close quarters with these people, the greater the likelihood I'll be caught.

"I have an idea," a nurse says. I glance away quickly. She's the one who caught me hacking the computers. She got a good look at me right before Dennis ran in naked and singing. I focus on the screen as she continues,

"If each interested patient writes down their dream spot to visit, do you think you could take them there with this thing?"

I nod. "Yup. Most of them."

"Yup..." She cranes her neck to look at me. "You seem so familiar."

"Yeah, well, you know, clowns. We're a dime a dozen."

"It's not that. Have you been here as a clown before? I can't place you."

I shrug.

Shouts erupt beyond the door, and the nurse reacts. She turns and moves toward the noise, ahead of the crowd. The whole room swivels, everyone heading out into the ward to see what's happening.

I'm in front of the crush, pushed through the door as staff scramble into the hallway. I swing to the side of the hall and press myself against the wall. I'm across from 218.

Becca's bed is empty. Her father stands at the door, wringing his hands.

"Is she okay?" I ask.

Even though it's a hospital clown asking the question, he nods. "She puts on a brave face, but she's so scared. It's the heart biopsy. She really hates it. I can't blame her."

"Wait—they take an actual piece of her heart?"

He turns to me. Eyes dark and clouded with fatigue.

"They make an incision in her neck, stick a giant needle down a vein, pinch four or five pieces of the heart and then yank the needle out."

"Holy…"

"Yeah." His focus returns to his hands. "We weren't prepared for any of this. Not even close."

I hear my father in him. *My one job.*

I'm silent for a minute while I think. What if Becca could be doing her favorite thing in the whole world? That would make all of this easier, wouldn't it? "What's something that she'd love?" I ask. "The wildest thing you can imagine?"

TWENTY-FOUR

By the time I reach Fatima, the PICU nurse has already called her with a list of places patients wish to see.

"Antarctica! Me too!" Fatima holds the list as she reads from it. "Do you know the story of Shackleton?" I offer a blank stare. "Marooned on ice, forced to launch a lifeboat across the Antarctic Ocean?" She clucks her tongue but then frowns. "Hey, this nurse who called is from the PICU. I thought we'd agreed to focus on the general pediatric unit." Her eyes search mine. "What's so interesting about the PICU?"

The best lie has elements of the truth. "My sister was in the PICU," I say. "I want to give back somehow. This seemed like a good way."

Her expression softens. "How's your sister doing?"

I shake my head. The pain rushes back, unexpectedly sharp.

"I'm sorry," she says.

"It's okay."

"Are you sure you want to keep doing this?"

"Yes."

She hands over the wish list, eyes understanding now rather than suspicious. "Well, maybe a virtual adventure will help. Not only will you be brushing up against the icebergs of the Antarctic, but you'll also be entering the Great Pyramid, climbing Machu Picchu and plumbing the Great Barrier Reef."

I scan the list. In addition to the ones Fatima mentioned, there's *Alien shoot-out*—this one, I'm betting, is from Tom. And at the bottom is *view from my rooftop*.

"Not sure I can do the last—the rooftop one." *Whose rooftop?*

"Do your best. I'm sure whatever you come up with will be better than nothing." She checks an iPad calendar. "Think you can have it together in a few days?"

"How's tomorrow?" I ask. She looks at me, surprised, so I quickly scramble to cover. "Jeannie told me that some of the kids don't have much time left." The truth is, I'm the one on borrowed time. Someone will unmask me soon.

"Okay, Emmitt. You're doing a good thing."

I force a smile. I'll convince Becca to be part of the video. I'll tell her it's for a school project or something— and then cut my losses. I can track her down again after she's out of the hospital and explain it all later.

On the subway, men and women sit or stand, sweating in their suits in the thick of afternoon rush hour. Must, mildew and body odor stifle the air in the older cars. The suits sway, unperturbed. They read.

Stare at the ads lining the bulkheads. Or listen listlessly through their earbuds. I wonder what everyone here would be doing if they had someone else's heart in them. Would they be walking home instead of riding on the subway, laughing at everything and giving passersby two thumbs-up for no particular reason but the glory of life? "I live!" they'd shout. "Me too! Isn't it amazing!" Would they be doing the same thing? *Would I?* This quest of mine feels important to me. But what comes after?

If by dying Minnie can save eight lives, what should I be striving to do by living? That's a high bar to hit. Joey wants to show his kids they don't need to follow his path. Eileen's playing bridge. Becca just wants to start her life. Dennis wants to celebrate...everything. Gerry's trying to spread goodness. I realize he's not tagging me on his posts anymore. I pull up his feed. I've missed a few. I like the one about a moth called the lettered sphinx. Shaped like a stealth fighter, it reminds me of Batman. Or perhaps I'm reading too much into Gerry's caption: **Put out the signal. Friends will come. #goodday.**

Would they come? I've noticed that I'm already closer to my organ family than any of my so-called friends. I wouldn't mind some positive distraction.

At home the hall is quiet and filled with cool shadow.

"Hey, Mom," I call. "I'm home." No answer. Silence. Not even the sound of the television.

I check my email for the hundredth time since I left the PICU, hoping my appearance made an impact on Becca yet dreading what it might have been. Disappointment flushes through me as I see that my inbox is empty. A text from Dennis. **So? Any luck today? I can't WAIT to meet her! <3**

"I'll start dinner. Have to make a quick call. Pasta okay?" My shout echoes in the empty hall. Empty house.

No response. I hum a dozen notes to fill the quiet.

I kick my shoes into a corner and shuffle toward my room, already dialing Joey as I go. Light flickers through the kitchen and living room entry, and I relax. The television's muted. Stockinged feet poke out from the end of the couch.

"Yeah," Joey answers. I turn from my mom and go into the bedroom.

"Hey," I say in a hushed tone as I shut the door. "Hi, Joey. It's Emmitt."

"Yeah, I know. Call display," he says.

"Well, thanks for answering then." Silence. "How are you doing?"

"Fine."

I'm left listening to his breathing for a few seconds. It's like a bad horror movie.

"I've got so much work to do tonight," I say. I boot up my laptop so I can start searching out experiences for PICU patients. I wonder what experience Joey would choose.

He asks, "Have you ever wanted something so badly it made you sick?"

I pause with my fingers on the keyboard.

On a blue plastic molded chair, I once offered *anything* for my sister to wake up. I've never wished for help so powerfully in my life. "Yeah. Yeah, I have."

"I feel that way about a drink."

Oh.

"You feel that way now?" I ask.

"It hurts. I don't think I can do this."

He's about to take a drink. But he hasn't yet. I close the lid on my computer.

"Joey, is your sister there? Your kids?"

"Out for groceries."

He's an hour away from me. I don't know what to do or say. I only have my promised questions. "Why do you want to live?"

Heavy breathing and then, "It's funny, but sometimes I wonder if I did the right thing."

"Answer the question." *Maybe he is.* I hate how lifeless his voice sounds, frayed and ready to snap.

"Before trying to make the transplant list, I could drink. Now I can't. I'm on all kinds of medications. Have all kinds of tests. I caught pneumonia. And I can't drink. What was the point of the transplant?"

I struggle to control the rage. "How will a drink help, Joey?"

He sighs. "Everything slips away. Because the choice is made. There's no more wrestling with it. Everything is easier."

A cap spins off a bottle and skitters on a table or a desk. I don't understand. I don't know what to say next. I only have my questions. "Why were you worthy of my sister's liver?"

A glass is poured.

"Was I worthy?"

No. "No." I squeeze the tears from my eyes.

"Right then." He draws a sharp breath.

The folds of my heart sister's letter lie accordion-shaped on my desk. *Careful not to foist your own ideals on others, right?* "But...wait! That's for you to decide, right? I mean, I don't want my sister's liver destroyed by booze. But it's not hers anymore, is it?" *And there it is.* A hot flush rolls over me. "It's yours now, and you have to decide what to do next." Joey is silent. "I was wrong. Minnie isn't your sponsor. I don't decide if you drink or not. *You* picked up my call, Joey. You answered. You don't want that drink. You want me to say something to stop you, but eventually you'll have to decide for yourself."

"It hurts."

I hold up the letter, scanning it for answers.

"But it doesn't always hurt, right? The pain waxes and wanes? You're scared. Scared. And drinking can take that feeling away."

"Yeah."

"How will a drink help you see how your kids turn out, Joey?"

"It won't."

"Why do you want to live?"

"To show my kids how to be strong." His voice is a whisper.

"So strong."

He breathes heavily into the receiver. "Do you think someone else died for me to live?" My grip tightens on the phone. He knows that's true. He *knows* that. "I don't mean your sister. I mean someone else waiting for a transplant."

"I don't know. Maybe."

I hear the glass slide onto the table. The cap slowly being screwed back on the bottle.

"Okay."

"Same time tomorrow?"

"Yeah. Thanks, Emmitt."

He hangs up. I don't know if it's enough. I stare at the phone screen for a moment before coming back to the depth of silence beyond my bedroom door. A truck rumbles past the house, rattling the chandelier in the dining room. I've let Joey go. I've let Minnie's liver go. Her eyes catch butterflies. Her lungs run.

I open my bedroom door and turn on the kitchen light. My mom hasn't moved from the couch. A bottle of pills is on the table. Tylenol. Was it there before?

"Mom?"

I poke her shoulder.

"Mom!" I shake her by the shoulders. Nothing.

I lean down, but I can hear only my own gulping breaths. Her chest rises and falls. I think. *There.* Her neck is cool under my fingertips. A wispy heartbeat.

I call my dad's phone, but there's no answer.

I text. **Can't wake Mom. I think she's taken a bunch of Tylenol.**

He responds. **9-1-1.**

I dial.

TWENTY-FIVE

I'm so sick of hospitals. This one's smaller. Older. Stuffy. I feel caged by unwashed privacy screens. My mother shares a room with another woman, her curtain perpetually drawn, her lungs perpetually trying to expel a lump of phlegm.

They don't think it was a suicide attempt. My mom took a few too many Tylenols but not a bottle full too many. Physical pain related to depression is rare but not unheard of, and the emergency doc thinks we'll be on our way home soon. She still needs to see a psychiatrist first. At least she has a bed and a room with only one other person.

My mom shifts but looks asleep. I don't think she wants to bother opening her eyes. She hangs out in the only room she can stomach. Lightless, hopeless yet carefree, a room bordered by her eyelids.

A knock comes at the door. I look for my dad, but he's not there. Another white coat.

"Hi, I'm Dr. Balder." He straightens his coat and touches his stethoscope with thick fingers. I relax at their sight. They're not surgical fingers.

I stand to leave.

"No, no." He glances at a chart. "Please stay, Emmitt. I hope you can fill in some gaps for me." His smile is warm. "Please."

I sit back down, and Dr. Balder pulls a chair from the other side of the curtain to sit beside me.

"I won't go over everything from the emergency room. I read through the notes. I'm sorry to hear about your sister."

I nod.

"Your mother suffers from depression. Do you understand what that means?"

I start to nod again, because that's what I'm supposed to do, but I stop. "I don't understand the difference between depression and sadness."

"It's a good question. The biggest difference is that sadness is tractable. That means it can be managed. It'll come in waves but will ease over time. It's part of the process of mourning. Depression, on the other hand, is intractable. Without medical help, it may take your mother almost a year to fully resurface from her illness."

My grief, when it comes, rolls raw and ragged over me and then is gone. I resurface after every wave. My mom stays down. I can't imagine it omnipresent, sucking, disorienting. I touch my mom's wrist. Her heartbeat is cool and flighty.

"But she wouldn't be depressed if my sister hadn't died."

"Grief is a common trigger of depression."

"A year?" I imagine fibers of the couch growing over her, a plaid lichen. That's how I'd film depression. Mundane yet terrifying. I picture an underworld fungus racing miles in every direction but showing only a single mushroom above.

"Nine months to a year, if left untreated."

My mom will lose her job. She'll lose her health. I look toward the psychiatrist. "And you can make her better?"

"I sure hope so, Emmitt. With your help."

Now the tightness in my gut reminds me of Joey needing his drink.

"But Emmitt, and this is important—"

I shift to the edge of my seat.

"—caring for someone is not the same as saving them. Do you understand?"

"Emmitt." My dad is standing at the door. I don't know how long he's been there, but only now do I catch the smell of tobacco smoke clinging to his clothes.

He flushes under my glare.

"Where were you, Dad?"

His fingers are tight on the door frame. "Been in the parking lot."

He couldn't come inside. The last time he entered a hospital, he lost his daughter. The fight that had surged in me breaks against the wall of his sudden vulnerability.

"I'm Dr. Balder." The doctor shakes my dad's hand, forcing him to remove his grip from the wall. My dad is still wearing his butcher's apron, which is crisscrossed with splatters of red, green and yellow. I imagine he was slaughtering peppers when he received my text. He rushed over but then froze in the parking lot. *The pain waxes and wanes.* It'll be better.

"Can we go home?" he asks. He twists his body to the hall, already on his way.

Dr. Balder says, "I can keep Allison here for observation, or you can take her home with her prescription, and I can follow her on an outpatient basis."

My dad enters and holds my mom's hand, her skin translucent with blue veins. His movements are jerky and nervous. I rise too. "We think she probably took seven or eight pills. We administered acetylcysteine, which is an antidote to this sort of overdose. It's likely that no permanent damage was caused to the liver. But she can have no more drugs of any kind, including alcohol, until tomorrow morning."

I glance up at the doctor. "My mom might have damaged her liver?"

"If your mom had taken any more pills, or you had waited longer to call the ambulance, then yes."

"By damaged you mean, like, need a transplant?"

"Possibly." I sense the blood draining from my face, the narrowing of my field of vision. "Sit, Emmitt." Dr. Balder takes me by the elbow and pulls me back into the chair. "She's going to be fine. Most people don't realize how dangerous acetaminophen is to the liver. How little it can take to scar it."

This time the cold that flows through me is that of realization. That there's no difference between my mother and Joey. Joey who destroyed his liver due to an addiction. My mother who nearly destroyed hers due to a depression. Both have illnesses. We were just lucky.

Dr. Balder speaks with my father and hands him a prescription to fill. Nurses remove the IV and monitors. Finally the room clears.

My dad and I help my mom out of bed and over to a wheelchair. It's not that she's catatonic, but she's like a puppet, and for now we need to hold the strings. For a moment I understand her. All I want is for someone to take over for me, to guide my strings, to keep me upright.

It's a long walk out of the hospital. And a very quiet ride home.

TWENTY-SIX

I go straight to bed when we get home. For the first few hours, I wake at the slightest noise, worried that my mom might be up and searching for pills to swallow. The refrigerator compressor starts. The water heater clicks on, followed by the whoosh of ignition. The furnace shuts off. Then the sounds begin to seem sinister. Padded footsteps. Creaking boards. A clink of silverware—*do people still steal silverware?* At 2:00 a.m. my feet slide onto the floor, and I creep over to my computer and bathe in its artificial light. I search out VR scenes from the wish list, head bobbing until I succumb to fatigue at 4:00 a.m., head nestled in the crook of my arm on the desk.

I wake to my phone rattling beside me.

The ringer's off, but it buzzes. Again and again.

I pick up the phone.

"I'm at your door." It's Dennis.

I look at the clock. Ten a.m.

I need to be leaving soon if I'm planning to do my rounds at the hospital. I spot an email from Martha. The subject: *You guys are so cute*. I pocket the phone before reading on, preferring to read Becca's emails with a level of intimacy that has been broken by my visitor.

I trudge to the door and open it a crack to reveal Dennis. He steps up, toes on the doorsill.

"Hi, Dennis," I say, holding the door half-open.

"Is she beautiful?" he asks, teetering.

"I've barely spoken to her."

"You've met her? You have! It worked? I knew it would work." He loses his balance and catches himself on the doorjamb.

"If you mean having to dress up as a clown and still be stared down by every nurse and doctor, then yeah, it's working well."

"Awesome. You have a picture? Can you text it to me? I'd love to meet her."

He talks like a machine gun.

"Listen," I say. "I really appreciate your help and everything, but my mom was just in the hospital and—"

"Oh." He steps down so that his face isn't in the door. He blanches. "Oh. I get it."

Guilt curdles in my guts. I know this has nothing to do with my mom. I know that.

"I guess she's not *my* heart sister, right? I'm more of an organ cousin, right? Once removed and all."

"It's not like that." *It is*, I realize.

Silence extends between us.

212

"Dennis, it's not like I don't appreciate your help, but you following me around all the time…it's a bit much."

Dennis folds his hands in front of him and stares at them as he says, "Six weeks ago my life changed forever. I'm still sorting out what to do with it. But you are too." When I don't respond, he adds, "You know where to reach me."

I shut the door and lean against it. Do I have any right to keep my heart sister to myself? I peek through the peephole. Dennis stands with his back to the house but doesn't leave. I yank out my phone and read Becca's email.

Email! We can email each other! I didn't realize my heart brother was a genius! OMG, now I can write you essays! Heart sister fan fiction. Oh, that's SUCH a good idea. I'm a genius. Let's collaborate on heart sister fanfic. What would she like it to be about? How would it start?

How can I let Dennis into the middle of this? I read on.

Speaking of fan fiction. Have you ever done fan art of your sister? Do any taxidermy? I mean, your sister loved it so much. I would think it would bring you closer. I could never. Needles. Blood. They're all problems for me. Most transplant patients get pretty blasé about people sticking things in them. Not me. I spend half my time panicking. Well, not about needles so much as big honking skewers in my neck—those I take issue with.

Okay, funny story—a clown came in today. Yes, you read that correctly—a clown. Not like Stephen King's It *type of clown. This was the real deal. Although he was a bit distracted and not all that funny, but cute, you know?*

I can work with cute.

Not that I'm at all interested, because he's a clown, and a weird one at that.

Must be less weird.

He comes in to show me his virtual-reality stuff. I'm really not into that. I have enough reality and prefer books for my entertainment. Don't you think there are enough ways not to talk directly with people in this world? I mean, they're talking about creating artificial-intelligence therapists. Can you imagine confiding in a robot for therapy? We'd need therapy for therapy, right?

You asked about awesome days. Well...I've never had an awesome day. That may sound selfish, given that the day I received a new heart was pretty awesome, but I wasn't pumping a fist after it, I was fighting for my life. An awesome day for me would be climbing to the top of the escarpment in my town without keeling over and looking back over the bay.

Here's your question of the day: what's the best thing that's ever happened to you? Mine (excluding the obvious heart upgrade!) will sound silly. But here it is. One time I was allowed to go for a sleepover. I was eight. They had a trampoline. My parents knew this, but they let me go because the parents had said that they'd watch and make sure nothing happened. But the parents went out on a date and left a babysitter, and we told her that we were allowed to bounce. I wasn't. It was glorious. I bounced until I couldn't breathe and my heart pounded. It hurt, and I loved it. Maybe that's fist-pump-worthy.

Love, YHS

She rambles less in her handwritten notes. I grin at the email. I feel as though I've gone way beyond sharing with Dennis. This feels so personal. I'm not too deflated by her lack of interest in virtual reality. I see it as a challenge. My dad is shuffling around in the kitchen, so I stay where I am and email Becca back, thumbs a blur on my phone.

Dear HS,

The best thing that's ever happened to me? You know, it's hard to remember good things. My sister is all I can think of these days. Anyway, I would say my favorite moment was this time around a campfire when we pictured our own personal dioramas. She sat there cross-legged and serious—I've never felt closer to her.

I have never dabbled in taxidermy. A sister who likes to skin animals is unusual enough. Pretty sure there are at least three frozen rats in our freezer still. But HS fanfic does sound pretty fun. I know she'd want her dioramas to come to life. I'll start.

As I sneak toward Minnie's room, I realize that what I said is true—I have never had any interest in taxidermy. It's not what I do. That's refreshing. Now her art will be the subject of my art.

After my dad trudges back down the hall, I tiptoe after him and duck into Minnie's room. The musty smell and the stream of sunlight igniting the whorls of dust motes remind me so much of Minnie, as if she's still here. Maybe she is.

I consider the massive diorama on the wall and soon realize that maybe Minnie was way ahead of me. Maybe this is a story already. It has the ingredients, the different planes of the sky, the city life and the underworld. I start typing.

Once upon a time, there was a little

I glance around for inspiration. I spot a mouse smaller than the others.

vole named Ivan. Like most voles, Ivan couldn't see worth a damn, but he had found himself a pair of magical glasses that allowed him to see things others could not. For instance, there was a skunk that regularly dove from the clouds.

I scan the diorama for more of the story.

But what the town feared the most was a five-headed monster rumored to live in the sewers. Kids were disappearing left and right from where they sailed on a lake and from the Walnut parking lot. Ivan suspected the rumors were the skunk's propaganda and set out to prove them fake and the skunk real.

Okay, your turn. Let's see if chaperone Martha will allow a photo.

I take a picture of the scene and attach it to my email reply. Outside the bedroom a door shuts. I duck out. From down the hall my father glowers at me in a don't-let-your-mother-see-you way but says nothing.

"How's Mom?" I ask.

"Eating. Drinking."

I nod. This is the starting line. I'll finish my video. That will sustain her.

Before hitting *send*, I go back to the email. I need my heart sister right now.

Thanks for calling me a friend. I thought I shared friends with my sister, but their going AWOL means that they weren't really my friends. I have a few I grew up with and then apart from. And others online that I have my art in common with, but really I have more in common with you than anyone. I mean, we don't know each other.

(That's a different thing to have in common.) We both share my sister. We both need someone to talk to about it all.

Here's your question. What's the worst thing that ever happened to you? You know mine.

Write soon.

I pause to decide how to sign off. I feel so close to her—not brotherly—but I'm confused as well. Becca is only my friend because of Minnie too. The walls of my blank room seem to press in. It's an email. I don't need to sign off at all. I hit *send*.

TWENTY-SEVEN

Before I'm allowed to deliver the wish list to the PICU, Fatima says I need to visit pediatrics. Despite being anxious to film Becca, I'm okay with the side trip because I've found something special for Joy.

I high-five the penguin and enter a nearly empty common room. I'd half expected the place to be clamoring with kids wanting to play video games. Only Isaac sits at his little homework desk. The crayons are out, and there is plenty of blank paper, but he hasn't drawn anything. I wonder about what Becca said, that technology is replacing social interaction and maybe other things. Isaac here used to scribble on any old piece of paper but can't anymore after drawing with starlight.

"Hey, Isaac, what do you say we draw together? You draw something, and then I'll add to it."

This feels like another collaborative story like that of Ivan the Vole.

"With the...?" He mimics putting on the headset.

"How about with paper? But I'll try to find a second headset, and maybe we can draw together another time." He sticks out his tongue and stares at his stomach. That's not good. I'm dressed as a clown, not a classroom teacher. "VR drawing it is!"

Isaac brightens and scrambles for the couch and TV.

"Where's Luke?" I ask.

"Surgery," Isaac offers before Jeannie can say anything.

"And Joy?"

"MIA," Jeannie responds.

I pause in my setup, the cord between the headset and console dangling from my grip. "Can you ask her a riddle for me?"

Jeannie raises an eyebrow but gives a grudging nod.

"What has six sides, can be opened with the mind, but means death in an hour?"

After I'm done with the setup, Isaac dons the headset and then grabs the hand controllers from the sack like he's done this a million times. I sit back and watch him paint a magical, impossible garden filled with sentient flowers, rocket-ship tubers and floating fruit pocked with doors and windows.

Fifteen minutes later Joy darkens the hallway.

"An escape room," she says. "That's the answer to your riddle. You need your mind to open it, but if you don't do it in time, you're dead."

In one hand she grips a green plastic basin. She starts to turn away.

"Wait!" Her step hitches but then continues. I call after her, "What makes a bow when cut off and runs white, blue and brown?"

She retches once into the bowl, doubled over. "A river...oxbow lakes form as the water cuts new channels," she croaks and shuffles farther down the hall.

"I have another—"

"Let me die in peace," she says, but she's half laughing. "I'm already cursed."

"Then what do you have to lose?" I'm guessing she cannot resist a puzzle. "It's okay. I bet you can't solve it anyway."

Joy groans and stares up at the ceiling.

"Isaac, give Joy a turn, buddy."

Isaac pulls off the headset and blinks around in disappointment at the distinctly unmagical setting.

"I want you to try this," I say. "It's an impossible mystery for the average human, but not for you. Come on."

"Two minutes." Joy squints at me but shuffles over and slumps onto the couch. I slide the headset over her bandanna. "Take this—and be ready," she says, handing me the basin.

There's vomit in it. It sloshes around, and I gag, holding it out with my arms fully extended. Jeannie swaps it out for a fresh basin.

The television screen shows Joy exploring an ancient Egyptian tomb.

"Okay, so I'm in some dead guy's house—keep that barf bucket handy. Just saying."

A granite slab slams down where the exit had been, and Joy jumps up off the couch, steadying herself with her arms out. "What just happened?"

A voice thunders, "You are doomed!" On the screen the room quakes, and sand sifts through the seams of blocks above. "You have until the glass is empty."

"Glass, what glass?" Joy pants, swinging left and right. "Oh my god. Oh my god."

"Check your pockets," I say.

She reaches down with the hand controllers and checks her imaginary pockets, pulling out a whip, a revolver and an hourglass. She turns it over, and a thread of sand begins to form a pile at the bottom. "What have you done to me?" Joy whispers.

The voice continues. "I am the Pharaoh Akhenaten, and I swear by my pointy chin that you have until the glass is empty to return the pieces of my mummy to the sarcophagus or face a painful death in the underworld."

"You know who will join me? Dappy the Clown. I'm superstitious about this stuff."

"You'd better hurry then," I say.

"Two minutes," she scoffs. Joy begins a search of the tomb, looking for clues. Over the next half hour, without asking for a single hint, Joy solves hieroglyphic riddles, shoots a grave robber, learns how to compute Egyptian math and theorizes on how the Great Pyramid was built. She crawls on the hospital floor, rolls to dodge a bullet, clutches her head as she concentrates.

In the final seconds, the ceiling slowly drops to crush her. Joy kneels, sliding the lid of the coffin closed as the last grains of sand fall to the bottom of the hourglass.

The voice of Akhenaten reverberates as the crushing ceiling stops and then retracts. "Thank you, child. May Horus ever have you under his watchful eye."

Joy lifts an arm in triumph and pushes up the headset, smiling right at me.

"You have another?" she asks. "'Cause bring it on."

She never asked for the basin.

TWENTY-EIGHT

My success with Joy renews my sense of purpose. I hustle over to PICU and try to convince Becca of VR's power. "I swear, VR can heal," I say.

"Really now," Becca replies.

"Not *heal* heal. Actually, maybe. Maybe temporarily. Definitely a positive distraction."

"That's conclusive. I'll try it again, but only if you have my wish."

"So which dream location were you? Ancient Egypt?"

"View from my rooftop."

Of course. The only one I couldn't really do.

"How passive-aggressive of you."

"It was my truth."

"Well, I think I can do better."

"I doubt that."

"Give it a try. If you don't like it, I'll never bother you with it again."

Her face turns serious, and she nods.

I set her up before she can change her mind. My heart beats a little faster as I touch her head to adjust the straps. To me, her skin has a bit of a yellowish tinge today. A bandage plasters her neck. Her hair smells of basil. I get goose bumps on my forearms when I brush against her hand. I watch as her arms prickle as well.

"Ready?" I ask, and she waves the controllers.

Although Becca is sitting in bed with my VR headset pulled down tight over her eyes, she stands virtually at the same spot Dr. Lebow did yesterday. It's not the rooftop Becca requested—it's the roof of the world.

Becca sighs and uses the hand controller to scratch at her forearm's IV line.

"It's nice, right," she says, a little louder than she needs to, calling over the harsh wind blowing in her ears. Her father isn't here, at least, so I feel we can speak more freely.

"Nice? The view from the top of Mount Everest is *nice*?"

"I didn't earn it. I think that's 90 percent of the beauty from a mountaintop."

"People don't earn their view of rainbows," I say.

"I'd wager that the view of the last rainbow you saw didn't change your life."

"But the view from Everest would, if you climbed it."

"If I'd accomplished something big like that, if I cared about that sort of thing, then yeah."

"So what do you care about like that?"

Her lips twist, as if wrestling with my question. Her hand creeps to the incision site on her chest.

"How was the biopsy?" I ask.

She takes off the headset and stares. "It's like having a hose shoved down your neck, that's how."

"Not bad then."

She snorts. "Yeah. Funny clown."

VR was a bust. I take back the headset and mull the silence as I repack the bag. "What do you want to do instead?"

"I dunno. Maybe talk?"

"I'm going into eleventh grade. Are you planning on being back in school this September?"

"We'll see. I try not to make plans."

"What's the first thing you want to do when you break out of here?"

Becca sighs. "I'm sorry. Maybe I'm too tired for conversation."

"I can do the talking. I already know I have a school project, a film. I'd love for you to be in it if—"

"No thanks," she says.

"What?"

"No. I really don't want to be some kid in a movie who everyone pities. And don't start a funding campaign for me either. One of my friends did that. It was awful. I don't know why people feel the need to share everything. She put my life up on a fund-me campaign. I need a heart that works for me—not money, not sympathy."

I want to explain the reason for my film. That it's not for the public. It's for her heart sister. For my mom. Maybe for me too. But I can't.

"Sorry," she continues. "I'm in a bit of a mood. Too many steroids. Do you mind?" She nods to the doorway. "I want to work on something."

She pulls a laptop from under her blankets and sets it on a table that swings in to sit just beneath her rib cage. I stand for a stunned moment before recovering.

"Your art?" I ask.

"Something like that."

As I finish packing my gear, she doesn't even look up. But she's grinning from ear to ear as she types.

I hesitate at the door, trying not to think about how I've failed. Her fingers tap at the keys. I'd give anything to have her grinning that way at me. I pull up the zipper on my bag and haul it over my shoulder, moving on to my next customer.

It's Nina. She's about eleven or twelve, and she wants the Egyptian tomb too. Bright-eyed and smiling with expectation, she doesn't seem long for the PICU. I'm about to ask why she's here, but then I see how the nub of her thigh lifts the sheet as she repositions herself. She's missing half of her left leg. I load the scenario.

Her head can barely hold up the gear as I lock it in place.

"I visited the King's Chamber last year," she says, turning her head this way and that. "I climbed into the sarcophagus and lay down like a pharaoh, like

Tutankhamun." She giggles. "I don't think you're supposed to do that, but my dad lets me do anything."

"That's pretty cool," I say.

"It was *amazing*. It was like everything else disappeared. Sounds became all wonky. My dad's words got hard to understand. And I started to hum."

She hums now. Judging by her ethereal tone, she's far away.

"My voice went up into these secret chambers above the ceiling and echoed back even louder. It's not working with this thing, but I really did. I'll never forget."

It's funny to me that someone's dream destination is a place they've already been, but the same is true for Rungha, who comes next—a skinny South Asian boy who wants to inspect an iceberg up close. Again it's as if he wants to share it with *me*.

In my search, I found icebergs as large as islands, vast shelves of ice, but the one I picked is a small one, weathered and full of small holes, shining in the bright sunlight.

"Sapphire," Rungha says. "That's what I remember the most. The color of pure ice."

Water laps at the side of the rubber Zodiac where the camera must have been perched. The ice seems to glow, as if carved by a surrealist sculptor, all hollows and sharp edges. Rungha chortles when three penguins leap out of the water, one after the other, to skim onto a shelf of the iceberg before sliding back into the frigid water.

"That looks so fun," he says and laughs as more penguins follow. "Chinstraps!"

He begins to take the headset off. "Not yet," I say, placing a restraining hand on Rungha's arm. He continues.

Quite suddenly the iceberg in the scene flips. At first it seems that it's rising, as if on the back of a great whale, but then the bottom, having melted to the point that the top is heavier, inverts in a massive crash of water. The Zodiac engine roars.

"Whoa!" A wave sends Rungha bouncing away. As the iceberg settles, light shines in a glorious blue tunnel. "That was so worth the wait. It is like the path home."

I swallow, pretty sure he's talking about death.

"Thank you," he says.

My bag vibrates.

"Your girlfriend?" he asks and smiles.

"Nah."

"I don't have a girlfriend either."

I don't know how to respond. He's probably fourteen or fifteen. Will he ever have a girlfriend? His skin is wan, and he's punctured by a half dozen tubes. I wonder what would be on everyone's wish list if they didn't have to choose a place. Would it be places to visit or experiences like flying? Or would it be to meet people? To experience having a girlfriend? To see someone one last time? I guess that's what I'm trying to do for my parents—to bring back the one person they most need to talk to.

It's getting late when I'm through. I don't want my mom to be home alone when my dad leaves for work. I rush to pack up. Going back past Becca's room, I see her with her fingers in her hair.

But I have nothing to say, no reason to enter. So I duck past and pull out my phone. Sure enough, there's an email forwarded on by Martha. The subject reads *Poor Ivan, I want to find out what happens next!* Martha has left the time stamp showing when Becca sent the email to her. It was just after my visit. *I* was Becca's project! If only she liked clown me as much as she does heart-brother me.

HB,

Oh, you ARE a storyteller. I'm happy-crying all over the place. LOL. Obviously, the angel-skunk is picking off mice and squirrel babies one by one. Okay, so Ivan wants to save these kid mice, and he's the only one who sees what's really happening. So he creates a map of all the crimes and triangulates them to figure out the hot spots where the angel-skunk is likely to land. It's all very vole-CSI.

After staking out the hot zone, Ivan watches the angel-skunk steal an unsuspecting mouse. He tries to save her, but he's just too small, right? And when he tells everyone about the angel-skunk, they just laugh him off. Who would believe in an angel-skunk? Obviously, it's a five-headed cat demon doing it. Over to you…

Clown's back. BTW, he actually asked me to be in a movie. That's a bit presumptuous, huh? I have to give the guy credit though. I heard people on the ward breaking out in laughter. You don't hear that much around here. I've been in a terrible mood. He hooked me up with a view from Mount Everest, and I'm all, like, whatever.

But it's really not stuff like that I feel like I'm missing. I'm missing out on things a healthy me will actually do. Like climbing onto my roof. Like investigating the alley behind the local bakery, or the huge storm drain that runs into the bay. That's what I want to see. I want to run down a hill as fast as I can.

To answer your question about the worst thing that's ever happened to me, PASS! Life's too short, dude. Here's a question for you: What is your greatest regret?

I have something I want to do before I kick it, something I don't want to regret not doing. Feel free to mock me, because I'm so beyond embarrassment. I want to kiss a boy. REALLY full-on make out—tongues and everything. Yeah. I'm seventeen and never had a proper kiss. Yeah. I'm oversharing. I can do that with you. Can I tell you one more thing? You can't joke about this though.

I'm scared.

I'll take a hug. I hear even virtual ones are still worth something.

YHS

I can't separate the welling in my chest from the girl in the next room. I know I have to, or I'll come across as insane, but all I want to do is…well…volunteer, I guess.

It explains why I couldn't sign my last note as heart brother. This feeling's a bit nauseating after calling her heart sister for so long. I've had girlfriends before. One that lasted a couple of months. But I don't think I've ever been closer to a girlfriend than I am with Becca. *What if I tell her?*

I shake the idea from my head. If I told her, she'd tell me off. I wouldn't have the star of my movie, and I'd likely be caught by hospital security and charged with trespassing and theft of medical records.

Still, I need to help her. She's scared. Scared of what?

I creep back to her door.

"Uh, hey," I say. "Just heading out and wondering if there's anything else I can do for you."

Becca smiles. "Uh, no, Dappy. I'm doing *really* well."

I press. "I was here yesterday for your biopsy." She scowls, and I rush on. "That sounds scary. The big..." I put my hand on my neck. "When's your next biopsy?"

She checks her phone. "Two hours, twelve minutes and five seconds...four seconds...three..."

"It's every day?"

"No. Yesterday's didn't happen because of my freak-out."

That explains her fear! I clap my hands and try to restrain my excitement. "I have an idea—I don't mean to be pushy. Sorry."

"Go on."

"I asked your dad what you would love, something wild. He said tigers."

233

"Okay. He was taking that very literally."

"How about kittens?"

"No, only tigers. Kittens I'd prefer to skin and wear as a hat."

I stare at her.

"I'm kidding!" she says. "But that's really funny if—never mind, it's an inside joke. Of course, kittens. What kind of serial killer do you think I am?"

"Right, okay then." I start pulling out my gear. "Will you try something for me? For your next biopsy."

"Maybe."

"I've got a kitten program."

"You promised, no more—"

"You can play with kittens while they're—"

"While they're shoving a hose down my jugular." She doesn't look convinced but then shrugs. "No promises."

"Awesome," I say. "I'll just leave it. Your call." I set it up with my computer so that all she has to do is slip on the headset.

She points her fingers at me like it's a gun and fires. I pretend I'm hit and stagger through the doorway.

Outside in the hallway, I keep my hands pressed over my chest. Then a familiar voice rings outs over the PA. "Code blue, room 212." That's just down the hall. Doctors and nurses converge on it as I sidle closer, hoping to slip past and out. But as I reach the room, it is strangely quiet. Doctors and nurses are standing around but just talking quietly. The heart-machine alarm is turned off. The boy lies unmoving. Where is the crash cart? The chest compressions?

Nurses filter out. One wipes a tear from her eye and continues in my direction. "Excuse me," I say. "What happened? Why aren't they saving him?"

The nurse gives me a compassionate smile and says, "Sorry, we really can't talk about other patients."

"Well, how do you know for sure he's dead even? I mean, with my—" I catch myself. "I mean, I hear there are all these tests they do, like pain, cranial nerve or ap...ap-something."

"Apnea tests?" she asks, and I nod. "Those are only in very special instances. When the patient is a potential organ donor."

"Wait a sec. If you want to be sure you're dead, I mean *dead* dead..." She gawks at me, and I blunder on. "What I mean is, if you want to be sure you're not going to wake up in your coffin underground, mistaken for dead, then—"

"Seriously, you're the least-funny clown ever, but yeah, register as a donor. The docs will make sure you're dead if you ever have the opportunity to have your organs recovered."

She leaves me stunned at the exit. I hear the click of Dr. Lebow's heels approaching the corner behind me. I hurry off the ward.

On the subway I contemplate for a moment how wrong I was during Minnie's testing. Their testing Minnie was the gold standard in assessing death. It wasn't opportunistic. If anything, to be a donor was a final chance, a last hope, for Minnie to do something powerful. Opportunity, the nurse said. The *opportunity* to be a donor. Unlucky in life, lucky in death. I recall my rage. My demand that she *breathe*. My rage hadn't been meant for the doctors. I was angry at Minnie. *Breathe*. For leaving me alone.

I write a response to Becca but get stuck at the salutation. I can't address her as heart sister anymore. I just can't. Right now I don't need my heart sister. I need Becca, and whatever we could be. For the first time in a long while, I detect a crack in the door to my future, and I sense her standing just behind it. I launch right into the message.

Hugs* *Virtual make-out session* What's the right make-out word? *smoochie* *smoochie* This is the best I can do. Something's definitely lost going from real to virtual, I think!

Seriously, I'm sorry you're scared. I can't imagine what it's like to have someone switch out a major organ. You're so strong! Another *hug.*

Every good story needs a reversal. Ivan the Vole, knowing he has no help, seeks to prove that the five-headed cat demon doesn't exist and that it can only be a diving skunk that is stealing the kids. He climbs down the hole of certain doom, only to find himself face-to-face with...the cat demon! Except she doesn't have five heads, she has seven! Dun-dun-DUN!

But the demon doesn't eat him. She wants a friend. Seizing the opportunity, Ivan recruits the cat demon—named Shelagh—to help stop angel-skunk and brings her to the surface, where they are met with needle-bearing mice! What happens next? Stay tuned to…you're up!

Answering your question: What's my biggest regret?

My mind flashes to Dennis's disappointed face this morning, but that's not it. That's just my most recent regret.

Never looking my sister in the eye and telling her I loved her. Never thanking her for all she did for me to make life easier and build friendships for me. Never saying goodbye to her. That's the one.

The more I fall for Becca, the less I can tell her. Family love burns like embers, and sometimes you can't tell if there's any heat left in the coals. But romantic love? I only know it from movies. A good director sets the scene. Condensation slides down a bottle of champagne. Music lifts and falls as fingers dance on ivory keys. Two gazes stretch across a room to meet, their hearts thrumming with the piano strings. If I want Becca to see me as more than a clown, more than a heart brother, I need to set the scene.

What's the most embarrassing thing you've ever done?

Of course, I can't tell her mine, because it's in progress right now.

TWENTY-NINE

I hop off the subway and for a second don't recognize where I am or why I'm here. It's too early for my stop. Then I realize that this is Dennis's stop. My conscience has carried me here. Maybe it was realizing how wrong I was during Minnie's testing. Maybe my letter to Becca brought me. I do know for what. To apologize. After all, he is my kidney brother.

I'll knock on his door, say I'm sorry and explain that Becca and I have a letter-writing relationship—it's not like it's love or anything real, but it's helping me, and it feels personal. He'll understand.

I'm on the sunny side of the street, and without the VR gear weighing me down, there's a bounce to my step for the first time in almost two months. This is the right thing to do. I push through the door to Dennis's walk-up and climb the stairs to his apartment. As I near his door, I hear voices.

So I text, I'm at your door.

Inside there's whispering and a sudden bang. The door before me creaks ajar.

"Hey, Dennis," I say, peering through the crack.

His head is cocked, eyes down.

"Hey, Emmitt." I can't tell if he's hiding something or if he's upset.

"Sorry, you know, about earlier." I'm taller than Dennis by a good six inches, and when I go up on my toes, I can see beyond his scalp. A green sheet lies flat on the floor. Furniture teeters against the side wall. *Painting?* I sniff the air and then continue, "It's just that—my talking to Becca is really helping me. I don't want to jinx it. I'm...I'm glad you followed me like you did."

"Okay, thanks. Bye." Dennis tries to shut the door, but I stop it with the toe of my shoe.

"Is someone over?"

He flushes.

"Do you have a girlfriend?" I whisper.

"Trust me, she's not my—it's not a girlfriend."

"Then..." I'm genuinely confused. What could he possibly be embarrassed about? The only other person we really have in common is—wait. "Eileen's here? The racist?"

Inside, another door swings open to clack against the wall. A woman says, "The one thing everyone seems to forget in the world today is that people can change."

Dennis rolls his eyes and backs up, opening the door wide to reveal Eileen standing there.

"It was supposed to be a surprise," Dennis explains.

"It is," I say. But then I spot the green sheet hanging against the back wall, overlapping with the sheet draping the floor. A camera is set up. An expensive one.

"I rented it," Dennis says.

"I still don't understand," I reply.

"You didn't have Eileen's video. For your film."

I glance at Eileen, who shrugs. "I'm sorry to hear your mom's ill."

"Why are you here?" I'd called her a "dead thing." That's a lot for her to claw back from.

"You said I could do better. I agree. I'm here to try." Her hair is up in a tight bun, and her face is just as pinched as ever, but there's a softness to her eyes. "Turns out we've known each other for a long while."

"You two?" I'm catching up.

"Insulin Junkie," Dennis says. "We were on the same diabetes forums together."

"I'd—of course—pictured him being a much older, strapping white man." Eileen snorts.

Dennis says, "I remembered all the questions, so thought I'd…"

After Becca's refusal, I know better than to turn down an opportunity. "Well, what are we waiting for?" I ask. "This is fantastic!"

Our high five cracks like a gunshot. Before he walks away, I grab his wrist. "Dennis?"

"Dude." He stares at my hand.

"Sorry. I just want to say thank you. For all of your help."

"It's nothing."
But we both know it's not.

EXT. CAMPFIRE - NIGHT

Around the campfire, MINNIE (16) sits with EILEEN (early 70s). Minnie has her guitar across her knees and plucks absently at the strings without realizing she's doing it. She grins at Eileen, face aglow, sparks flying into the night.

MINNIE
What's your name?

EILEEN
Eileen.

MINNIE
If you were an animal, what would you be?

Eileen eyes the camera as if it's a snake.

EILEEN
A mule.
(laughs)

When I was little,
I rode horses out on
a farm. A working farm
with other animals.
I refused to ride
any other horse but
a white mare. The
trainer said I was
like a mule.

MINNIE
If I were to put you
in a diorama, what
would it look like?

EILEEN
Oh, I'd be braying at
someone or something.
I enjoy telling people
where they are wrong,
see. I'm only trying
to help.
        (beat)
My diorama would
have a bunch of sad
piglets, cringing in a
pigsty as I tell them
to clean up.

243

> ### MINNIE
> Cool. What would other people put in your diorama?

Eileen's squint tightens.

> ### EILEEN
> I know who I am. I know people think I'm a busybody. Unwanted. No longer useful, if I ever was.

Eileen's eyes shimmer with anger and perhaps shame.

> ### EILEEN (CONT'D)
> They'd have the same diorama, but maybe someone would have tied something to my tail. A balloon—something I can't shake off. They'd mock me, see?

> ### MINNIE
> How can you make the diorama better?

Eileen sighs. This is the tough
one for her. Changing.

> EILEEN
> I don't know. I can
> ignore the pigs and
> their mess. Why
> do I care? Maybe
> that's just what pigs
> do? Maybe I can bray a
> bit less. Maybe
> there's a horse in me,
> like I'm a pony who's
> decided to be a mule
> and can decide to be
> a horse again.
> (swallows)
> This isn't easy for
> me today, coming
> here, but...organs—
> I've looked into this.
> An organ doesn't care
> what body it's in. All
> the same stuff. All the
> same.

Eileen's eyes sparkle with
emotion.

> FADE OUT.

Silence stretches out. My finger rests on the Stop Recording button.

"We done?" Eileen asks.

"That was so brave," I say finally.

"Thank you to Minnie," she says.

"To Minnie," Dennis agrees, clutching his side. "And to my organ twin."

Eileen winces, her lips a white line, and then she relaxes a bit. "To my organ twin."

I'm still filming.

"You know what I think about sometimes?" Dennis says to Eileen. "It's how my kidney isn't really a kidney at all. It's like the Triforce."

Eileen looks at me.

"No idea what he's talking about," I say.

"From *The Legend of Zelda*."

"Still nothing," I reply.

"Okay, not the Triforce then. My kidney and my pancreas are like diamonds the size of my fist. Seriously, think about this. Here's what *actually* happened. I had my operation in Hamilton. Three surgeons from Hamilton got offered the organs by the National Transplant Organization. Using a super-complex algorithm in some high-tech operations center, they decided Minnie and I were a match. The surgeons drove to Toronto with a team of people, where they removed the kidney and pancreas. Evidently surgeons usually do their own organ recoveries."

As Dennis explains, my chest tightens again.

"They packed the organs, and then they, not a courier but the actual doctors still, carried them to a helicopter or a waiting van, which rushed them all to Hamilton. In Hamilton the streets were blocked off by police as the organs traveled across the city, as if it was for the president or something. All of this timed to precision.

"Meanwhile, a team of people prepped me. The same surgeons who recovered the organs performed the operation on me. At this point they'd been working for hours and hours. These people, with their years of experience and education, devoted their day to me. After the surgery another team spent a week with me in the intensive care unit. And for who?" He stares at each of us.

"See? They're not a kidney and a pancreas. Diamonds. Life. And just like Eileen said, and like the Triforce in *The Legend of Zelda*, it gives life indiscriminately. Who am I? I'm just Dennis, some kid who wants to code software. I had a great-uncle who couldn't bring his family over from China because the government had slapped a head tax on them. He was so lonely. Lived in a rooming house for two decades. He thought he had no value. But they put big honking diamonds in his great-nephew. Don't you see how spectacularly crazy that is? That's the most amazing thing in the world."

I swipe the tears from my cheeks. It's more than Dennis's story though. Minnie was treated like a queen too. I was so wrong. When Minnie arrived at the hospital, they spent hours trying to resuscitate her. They put her on life support. The doctors did their tests for death. We were given the option. Did we wish to have her moved to a funeral home, or did we want to try to save eight lives? Did we want to bury eight diamonds?

Minnie was never coming back. In the ground those diamonds would turn back to coal. While the doctors were recovering her organs, they treated her with all the respect given to a live patient. Even though she wasn't. She had died out on the street in front of that car.

Dennis shakes his head at me, as if still unable to believe his luck. Eileen watches him contemplatively.

"I have to run," I say.

"I'll send you the video, okay?" Dennis says.

As I close the door behind me, I glance back at Eileen, who looks at ease in the strange apartment.

Walking briskly to the subway in the heat, sweat beading on my brow, I call Joey. He's having a better day, and by the time I hang up, I'm feeling closer to my organ family than ever. If only I could stop thinking of Becca with a needle stuck in her neck.

THIRTY

Becca must have snuck in a final email before Martha left for the day. In the subject line Martha writes, *Smooches!*

> *HB*
>
> **smoochie?* *smoochie?* Really? Maybe I need to lower my expectations on this kissing stuff. Besides, you're my heart BROTHER. *gags**
>
> *Sounds like you have a mission though. I gotta wait for my boy to show, but you don't have to wait to tell people you love them. Maybe it is too late for your sister, but not for anyone else in your family. It's an awkward feeling, I know. I told my dad I loved him right before I went into surgery. And not an off-the-cuff "love you, big daddy-o." I held his gaze and I said goodbye, just in case. Don't wait.*
>
> *Are we closing in on the climax of Ivan the Vole and the Cat Demon? The epic saga continues! Ivan faces the mice crowd (do they have to be armed with needles?*

You're giving me nightmares!) and tries to tell them the truth about the angel-skunk—who, he has determined, will strike at any moment but several blocks away. The crowd won't listen and begins stabbing Shelagh in the necks, again and again. Ivan urges her to fight back, but she won't. Can't. She's been in the sewers all her life. Ivan struggles in the clutches of half a dozen mice. Finally Shelagh only has one head left, and she starts to retreat to the sewers. What's Ivan to do?

Okay, so I honestly don't know. It's all yours. And I need to send this before Martha checks out. My most embarrassing moment though? That's a tough question. I don't have a good enough answer yet. I'll get back to you.

I'm running out of questions to ask, but here's another. For one million dollars: Your house is on fire. What one thing do you save? (Other than your family, duh.)

YHS

Becca didn't mention how the biopsy went. Maybe she hasn't had it yet. But she *has* sent me on a mission. She's right. I have no excuse for not having told my parents I love them. Why haven't I? Is it *too* real? Is my movie of Minnie a virtual *I love you*? A just-in-case goodbye?

I step into the house. The rapid-fire chopping of my father dicing vegetables ricochets down the hall. When I shut the door, the knife stops.

"That you?" he asks.

Don't wait.

"Yes," I say, my breath catching in my throat. When no further conversation is forthcoming, I pop off my shoes and slowly walk down the hall, the snap of the blade on the cutting board covering my footfalls.

At the kitchen and living area, I pause. Dad keeps chopping a carrot into ever smaller pieces.

"It's dead," I say.

My dad sighs and gives me a don't-push-me-son look before mincing the carrot more. "I have to go into work. I'm making burgers."

The stainless-steel bowl before him is filled with minced vegetables. He'll cook them and form them into patties. With seasoning, it actually tastes pretty good.

"Today I made hippos from potatoes and orcas from cucumbers," he adds.

He stops as if to gauge my reaction. He's waiting for me to call them hippotatoes and orcucumbers. Instead I leave silence.

"That makes sense," I say. "Food tastes better when it looks good, right? Or looks like large mammals."

He snorts. The knife again rocks dangerously close to fingertips.

He knows I love him. I don't need to say it. It's *why* we don't say it.

"Maybe we can watch a movie this Friday," I say.

"Big wedding to prep for on Saturday."

Chop, choppity chop, chop.

"Dad..." His gaze lingers on the granules of carrot. "I love you."

He gives tiny nods, like the mincing nods of his blade. He looks away, but the knife hits warp speed.

"No, Dad," I say. "Can you look at me?"

He cries out, whips away his hand and inspects it. "Hit a nail." He blows out a sigh.

"Dad. Look at me." His head slowly lifts. "In the eye." Our gazes meet and hold. After a moment his eyes begin to shimmer. "I love you, Dad."

The chopping nods resume.

"Thank you, Emmitt," he whispers. His chin drops, and a tear spatters on the cutting board. He picks it up with his apron. "I love you too."

Chop, choppity chop, chop.

The corners of my lips drag lower. It's an uncomfortable, uncontrolled, uncertain emotion. Relief? Grief?

I'm biting my lip as I turn away and walk over to my mom.

She doesn't look up, eyes transfixed by the flashing pixels of light on the TV. I kneel before her, but her eyes stare through me to the screen.

I turn off the television, and her focus doesn't change. She wasn't really watching anything. I crouch lower so that I can at least look her in the eyes. I wonder if I'm being selfish. Having to tell people I love them rather than just showing it. Forcing my love on them. Isn't the rule the same for love as it is for storytelling? Show, don't tell?

"Mom." Her gaze wavers, eyelids drooping. Her green eyes seem gray in the gloom. I hope it's just the light. "I love you, Mom."

The flatness of her eyes scares me. No tears. No smile. Her gaze shifts to the slate TV screen in anticipation. We are reflected in it. A muted, fuzzy echo of what we've become. I turn it back on, feeling hollow. I drape my arm over her bony shoulders and squeeze, but not hard. She is so fragile.

When I stand, my dad's gone with the bowl. Off to work to shape veggie burgers. There's blood on the cutting board. He nicked his finger after all.

Maybe I waited too long to tell my parents I love them. But it's done.

If I were Ivan the Vole, I'd sit on the ground, curl up and cry. Not a great ending for our story, huh? I wonder if writers' endings change with their moods. I'm not sure I'm up to writing about a hero. This must be my darkest hour. If there was a fire in my house, I wonder if we'd even save ourselves. Or just let it all burn. To ash. Okay, I'll try. Here goes.

Ivan slinks back into the underworld with the cat demon and huddles in the dark, listening to Shelagh's whimpers. All the while, he knows another mouse has been taken. Perhaps he could make a life for himself here in the darkness, he thinks. Shelagh had. But then he arrived, and now Shelagh has only one head, and it's all his fault. He can't ask her to help again. He realizes it's all up to him. It always has been, really. Knowing that, he makes a plan. He must catch angel-skunk.

Clambering back to the surface and his maps, he plugs in the latest locations of the missing mice. He must hide now, as the others believe he is in league with the evil cat demon. Ivan must set a trap. He will be the bait.

I'm scared too. I'm scared for Ivan and for my family and whether we'll ever be a family again.

The letter is almost too sad to send.

What would I save from the burning house?

I consider the options. My VR gear? Pictures of our family?

*"Rat Race." My favorite diorama of my sister's.
It reminds me to enjoy the journey.
I don't have a question for you, only some advice.
To take your own advice. You may not think you've met your boy yet, but are you looking hard enough?*

<3

I hit *send*.
This time I know I'm being selfish, but I can't stop smiling.

THIRTY-ONE

"Dappy!" Becca cries, and her father waves me into the room.

"There he is." He takes me by the elbow and pumps my hand.

I stand confused, arm waggling, and then I get it. "It worked? Your biopsy?"

"When you said kittens, I didn't realize there would be so many!" Becca laughs, and suddenly the fluorescents shine like sunlight, and the machines chirp like birds. "A wriggling mass of *cuteness*!" She hugs herself.

Her father motions to his chair, as if it's a place of honor.

"I'm so happy," I say. Today Becca sounds like she does in her letters.

"At first the doctors were, like, no way. But then I was, like, no way about the whole needle-neck-vein thing. And so they talked about it, and one of the nurses spent, like, an hour disinfecting your plague-bearing apparatus before revving it up, and, well, they covered me, froze the area, cut open my vein and stuck me, and when they were done, they said I was smiling most of the time."

"That's a pretty big difference," her father says.

I lean over the bed and give her a fist bump.

"I'll do your movie thing," she says.

"My what?" I ask.

She looks at me, eyes bright. "Your film! I'll be in it."

"Oh!" I have the star of my movie. The show will go on!

I don't waste a moment. You shoot when your cast is available. My makeshift green screen unfolds, and I struggle to tuck it in behind her. Her father helps. Then I duct-tape a green sheet to the wall—a good director always has a roll of duct tape stowed. When I'm ready, she's wringing her hands.

"I know it's just a school project, but...don't...don't put it out *there*, okay?"

Even though I'm worried that I'll spoil the moment, I ask, "On the internet, you mean? I wasn't planning to, but—just curious—why not?"

"I don't think I could handle the comments. People telling me to fight. How I can *do* it. The congratulations." She swallows hard.

"Okay," I say. "I promise."

EXT. CAMPFIRE - NIGHT

Around the campfire, MINNIE (16)
sits with BECCA (17). Minnie has
her guitar across her knees and
plucks absently at the strings
without realizing she's doing it.
She grins at Becca, face aglow,
sparks flying into the night.

          MINNIE
  What's your name?

          BECCA
  Becca.

          MINNIE
  If you were an animal,
  what would you be?

          BECCA
  A...dragon.

          MINNIE
  If I were to put you
  in a diorama, what
  would it look like?

          BECCA
  These are different

> questions than I
> was expecting. My
> diorama...odd. My donor
> made dioramas.

I didn't even consider that she might make the connection. I try to look surprised by the unlikely coincidence, and she moves on.

> Becca looks down at where
> the incision is in her chest.
> Beneath the gauze, heavy black
> stitches hold her together.

> BECCA (CONT'D)
> In my diorama, I
> am in a battle. I
> protect a magic stone
> from clawing demons.
> They're coming from
> all sides. One even
> has a talon digging
> into the stone.

> Becca chokes up a little.
> This has been a long fight.

> MINNIE
> Cool. What would other
> people put in your

diorama?

           BECCA
Maybe the dragon is
painting? It's funny,
because people always
saw my bad heart,
because that was on
my face, and it was
the creative force
behind my online
persona, Dark Heart.
Now? Now I don't know.
What else do I still
have to offer? Will my
art be as powerful to
them when they realize
I've got a heart just
like theirs? I think
people will see an
artist-warrior on a
dragon. Triumphant
and standing over
her magic stone.
That's what they will
see. That's what I've
always shown people.

Becca smooths out her hospital
gown.

BECCA (CONT'D)
So far.

MINNIE
How can you make the
diorama better?

Becca smiles sadly.

BECCA
I'm just starting my
quest. I don't know. I
don't know. I'd hoped
by now I wouldn't
have to look over my
shoulder and see Death
or drag wires around.
The battle would
be won. I would be
unchained...unchained.
But for now, I still
wonder if I'll have
a chance to make
anything better.

Tears stream down Becca's face.

BECCA (CONT'D)
Maybe the heart
should have gone to

someone else? Maybe...?

Becca's eyes sparkle with
emotion, and Minnie grins.

FADE OUT.

"Shh...shh..." her father murmurs, comforting her. His eyes implore me to leave. "It's the steroids," he explains as I pack up the camera as quickly as I can. "They cause big mood swings, anger, sadness." He hugs her and says to me, "Come back tomorrow."

I leave Becca lying on green sheets. Green so that I can place her in any environment I want, a paradise or a hell, with Death at her shoulder, a magic stone at her feet or a campfire in June. I see the control over my life that I've always had, control that she has never tasted. Trust she has placed in me. I struggle with the whiplash of emotion. Can what I've done be justified? Heat flushes through me as I realize it can't.

I don't go home. For the rest of the morning I visit the pediatric ward and strive to be Dappy the Clown, trying to shed guilt like a snake sheds skin.

On the subway home, I realize I have everything I need to help my mom. All that's left for me to do is edit the videos...just right.

THIRTY-TWO

Editing video is finicky but critical work. So much of the story is created at this stage. I have to constantly keep my audience in mind. What do my parents want to see? How much reality can they handle? Editing 360-degree video requires specialized software that I'm still learning. I can't keep all of the content. Some I don't want to keep. Some I can't bear to part with.

It takes a week's worth of swearing and hair pulling before I'm remotely happy with it. And my laptop doesn't appreciate having to manipulate multiple high-definition camera feeds. It hangs up four times. I save regularly, but not regularly enough.

Finally I hit *render*, allowing the video to process overnight, fingers crossed that the laptop can keep up with it. Then I crash out face down on my bed and don't have a single dream.

I wake to dull light seeping around the curtain edges. I look at the clock. Just before nine. I've had five hours of sleep, but I leap up like I'm four years old and headed for a stocking on Christmas morning. I wake the computer, pump my fist at the *Render successful* notification and slam the headset over my eyes and ears to enter the scene starring my heart sister.

```
EXT. CAMPFIRE - NIGHT

Around the campfire, MINNIE
(16) sits with GERRY (late
50s), DENNIS (early 20s),
EILEEN (early 70s), JOEY (mid-
30s), BECCA (17) and EMMITT
(16). Minnie has her guitar
across her knees and plucks
absently at the strings without
realizing she's doing it.

          EMMITT
        (voice-over)
   This summer Minnie
   sat me down at the
   campfire and asked
   some questions.
   Then she shared her
   answers to the same
   questions. I made this
   so that you would
   know Minnie lives. Not
   as the person
```

we knew. But not only
as a memory either.
Rather, she lives on
in the people who
received her life-
saving organs. Our
extended family.
>   (beat)

Our first character
needs no introduction.
Here's Minnie with her
first question.

>   MINNIE

If you were an
animal, what
would you be?

>   EMMITT

Every family member
has a different
answer. Let's go meet
everyone. Like Gerry,
her corneas.

>   GERRY

Calm in battle. Sharp
in sight. A mongoose.

EMMITT
Eileen, her left
kidney.

EILEEN
I am a difficult
woman. A mule.

Minnie laughs.

EMMITT
Joey, her liver.

JOEY
A ferret. With two
little ferrets.

EMMITT
Dennis, her other
kidney. The one on
the right. And her
pancreas.

DENNIS
I am a spotlight
whipping across
the landscape,
highlighting
the amazing. I
am a barista

extraordinaire! An
orangutan.

EMMITT
Minnie's lungs went to
a woman who doesn't
want to talk, but we
know that she'll be
racing in this year's
Transplant Games.
Running. And now able
to keep up in the rat
race.
(beat)
Becca received
Minnie's heart. She's
your heart daughter.

BECCA
A...dragon.

Minnie grins, face aglow,
sparks flying into the night.

MINNIE
If I were to put you
in a diorama, what
would it look like?

GERRY

My coat, a big trench
coat, would be on the
ground for a lady
mongoose to step on,
and I'd be tipping my
hat in appreciation,
watching all the other
mon—what's the plural?
Mongeese?

JOEY

Easy. Face down in the
dirt. Tiny bottles all
around. One still in
my hand. Two little
ferrets staring on.

DENNIS

I can finally define
myself without being
defined by illness.
Maybe there's just
this spotlight on me
and a director person
just said, "Action!"

EILEEN

I'd be braying at a
bunch of sad piglets,

cringing in a pigsty
as I tell them to
clean up.

BECCA
I am in a battle.
I protect a magic
stone from clawing
demons. They're coming
from all sides.

EMMITT
Everyone here has
faced challenges
to be a recipient.
Challenges that would
have buried many
people. Blindness.
Addiction. Isolation.
Long, long illness.
A piece of them has
died with Minnie
too. And now they're
figuring out how to
live again. In a
strange way, Minnie
stuffed them, and
now they're figuring
out their own new
arrangements.

             MINNIE
Cool. What would other
people put in your
diorama?

             GERRY
Geez. How do they see
me...

Gerry's mouth tightens,
and he glances down at his
hands, hands that have pulled
triggers.

             GERRY (CONT'D)
They'd put me on a
rooftop with a clear
line of sight for my
scope.
             (beat)
I've got a lot of
brothers, sisters,
moms and dads to
answer to in the next
life. I did my job—
saved and protected
many more people
than I shot, but some
people will only ever

see a killer.

Gerry's shoulders slump, defeated.

              JOEY
     There would be
     more ferrets. Other
     animals. Cats, dogs—
     they'd be protecting
     me, even though I'd
     eat them if I could
     stand.

Joey looks up, surprised.

              JOEY (CONT'D)
     Lifting me. One might
     be putting another
     bottle in my hand.
     They'd be hugging me.

              DENNIS
     Whoa! You know what?
     I bet I'd be this sick
     gamer to them. They
     don't know me, not
     physically. The ones
     who did, they'd see me
     as a kid in a hospital

bed. But that's over.

Eileen's squint tightens.

> EILEEN
> A busybody. Unwanted.
> No longer useful.

Eileen's eyes shimmer with anger and perhaps shame.

> BECCA
> An artist-warrior on a dragon. Triumphant and standing over her magic stone. That's what I've always shown people.

Becca smooths out her hospital gown.

> EMMITT
> An organ transplant is a near—death experience. I don't know another way to put it, but Minnie and all the doctors and nurses are like

angels, offering
another chance to
change.

          MINNIE
How can you make
the diorama better?

          GERRY
When I see something
new, learn something
I never knew before,
that's a good day.
I don't think I can
fix the diorama, not
the one others see.
Just mine. There's a
reason why I chose
the mongoose as my
animal. They're immune
to snake venom. Eat
cobras for breakfast.

Gerry's jaw flexes, much as it
did on a mission, just before
he relaxed to take the shot.

          JOEY
I need to get out
from the hugs, right?

I need to push myself
up onto my knees.
Brush myself off.
Stand. Show the two
little ferrets I can
be strong myself.

Dennis's chin tilts upward.

                DENNIS
Orangutan-me is gonna
hang from the tree
branches and swing,
and collect durian
fruit or termites or
whatever they eat, and
use my super-amazing
fingers to code even
faster. And when I'm
done, I'm gonna donate
my organs! And if I
don't die when they're
still useful, I'll give
them money, because
every moment from here
on out I owe to the
kind stranger who gave
it to me. I owe you.

Dennis laughs.

Eileen sighs. This is the tough one for her. Changing.

> **EILEEN**
> Maybe I can bray a bit less. Maybe there's a horse in me, like I'm a pony who decided to be a mule.

Becca smiles sadly.

> **BECCA**
> I'm just starting my quest. Now...unchained.

Tears stream down her face.

> **EMMITT**
> Minnie's here still.

> **EILEEN**
> Thank you to Minnie.

> **DENNIS**
> In me they put big honking diamonds. Don't you see how spectacularly crazy that is? That's the most amazing thing in

the world.

                    EMMITT
We celebrate quick-
thinking people who
save others in a
moment of crisis. But
people who, in the fog
and agony of grief,
can think beyond
themselves despite
crippling pain? That's
the ultimate kindness.
I couldn't do it. I
didn't. You did. You're
the heroes. It's what
Minnie wanted. And
it's BIG. So big.
          (beat)
She's a catalyst for
change, for love, for
determination, for
family, improvement,
for new beginnings,
and that's all she
ever wanted. But don't
take it from me...

                    MINNIE
I'm Minnie. A unicorn.

```
My diorama has this
cool, smart owl of a
mom, and a bear dad
just crazy enough to
inspire me. I'm a twin
to my best friend, a
fierce and loyal mouse
named Emmitt.
I can make the
diorama better every
day by giving it my
all. That's all it can
ask of me, and all I
can ask of myself.
```

```
Minnie grins through the fire.
```

```
                        FADE OUT.
```

My breath comes in short gasps, and I taste blood on my lip from biting down on it. I'm so proud of her, but I can't shake the feeling that she jinxed herself somehow. That the universe took her oath too literally. *I will change the world by giving it my all.*

I pull off the headset, my hair sweaty and tousled, my cheeks tear-soaked. I place the headset on the shelf, beside the turned-down picture, the one of Minnie and me cliff jumping. My fingers brush the frame. I can't flip the picture. Not yet. I can watch Minnie's VR all day, but I can't look at a static image of her.

I bend to the butcher paper and shade in all the colors of Becca's rainbow heart. I'm not fully satisfied with the video. It's not the syrupy, positive piece I'd first imagined—not Disney's version of Minnie's impact. But I think it's the amount of cutting I needed to do for Becca's part that bothers me the most. Maybe it's the steroids, but something isn't right. I feel like I left too much of her on the cutting-room floor.

I think I had to for my mom's sake.

I take a final look at the drawing of Minnie and her organs, and after a long blink I roll her up, fold her in half and slide her into my hockey bag with the rest of my superhero memorabilia.

Then I take my headset, the weathered laptop and the hand controllers into the living room, where I plug it into the TV. It's time. It's *my* all.

THIRTY-THREE

I set it all up before I bring my mom to the living room.

"Mom, I have something I'd like you to watch." She has never been keen on virtual reality because it makes her nauseous. "It's short, and there isn't any movement involved, so I think you'll be okay." Her face remains flat. "You'll really like it. You need to watch this, okay?"

When I bring the headset toward her, she doesn't resist. "I need to warn you though. Minnie is in it. I know it will be hard. But I hope this makes you sort of sad-happy, okay, Mom? Okay?"

I ease her onto the couch and grip her hand in mine.

"Here we go." I swallow and hit *Enter VR*, and my mom joins the campfire.

"*This summer Minnie sat me down at the campfire and asked…*" VR me begins, but I'm only half listening. As the experience starts, my mom shakes her hand free of my fingers and reaches up to pull the headset tighter to her scalp.

"…here's Minnie with her first question."

My mom's fingers tighten on the headset, and her legs swing off the sofa.

I start to grin as she takes a couple of stumbling steps toward the TV. She's up, wobbling like a fledgling on an unsteady test flight. Her face holds more hope than I've seen in weeks. Her back and knees start to bend, and I realize she's not walking toward the TV. No matter who is talking, she focuses on only one part of the scene.

"Minnie," she whispers.

"Mom, it's just a video," I say.

But she's not listening to me. She's listening to her daughter.

"*If I were to put you in a diorama…*" I watch Minnie on the TV.

My mom kneels before virtual Minnie and reaches out.

But her hands pass through her daughter. I know they are passing through nothing, and beneath the headset that covers her eyes and upper cheeks, my mom's mouth twists.

"Minnie!" she shouts and wraps her arms again and again around nothing at all. "Minnie!"

"Mom!" I shout to break through, but she's not here. I unplug the VR gear, blinding her.

"No!" she screams.

She gropes the air, hitting the TV, which rocks on the wall. Her fingers pull off the headset, and her eyes search the room.

"Where? Where is she?"

And I realize something is very wrong. Her eyes are wild, unfocused. She gets to her feet and runs, me trailing, to Minnie's bedroom.

"Minnie?" she calls as she opens the door.

I can't help but listen for an answer too.

Once inside there's a moment of peace on her face. Minnie's room is just as it's always been, so everything must be fine. Then she runs a finger across a shelf.

"Why is it so dusty in here?" She paws at the shelves, knocking over mice and squirrels, scattering nuts. "Minnie usually keeps this all so tidy. Where's your sister, Emmitt?"

I try to be strong as I answer, but my voice cracks as I say, "She's dead, Mom. She's dead."

I've made a terrible mistake. My mom was not ready to hear about Minnie living on, giving life to others. She collapses to the floor, sobbing.

Later, when my mom's back in her bed, looking worse than ever, my dad tries to comfort me. "It's okay, Emmitt. You didn't know. She'll come around. The doctor said the medications take at least a week or two to begin having an effect." But I can't help but wonder if he's staying home from the shop today to protect her from me.

I leave them together and trudge alone to my bedroom. I text Dennis. The video didn't work. My mom freaked out.

He sends a sad emoji, then: Can I see it?

Sure. How about we give it a day though.

Eileen will want to see it too. We all will.

I know.

There's a pause during which I can practically feel him wrestling with whether to show up at my door. Finally: Tomorrow then. I'll see you tomorrow.

They will all want to see it—Gerry, Eileen, Dennis, Joey.

Joey.

Crap, I totally forgot to call Joey last night. I spent all my time editing the video. I punch in his number immediately, but it goes to voice mail. My inbox has no messages from Becca. I debate whether to send her one, but all I want to talk about is my mom and the video and how it didn't work. Maybe I can go see her.

When I walk back into the kitchen, I spot my dad cutting onions. He wears goggles to deal with the stinging mist. With the knife and the goggles, he looks like a guard.

"I'm heading out," I say, and I note the relief in his shoulders. "Will you watch the video I made of our organ family?"

"Maybe," he says. I realize he's been crying even with the goggles on. "I'm not sure I'm ready for it either."

Back at the PICU, as I approach Becca's room, I feel unarmed. I'm in my clown getup, but Dappy doesn't have his VR system today. I left it at home with my dad, hoping he'll watch the video and have a different reaction from my mom's. *Maybe.*

"Hiya, Dappy!" Dr. Lebow waves, and I grin back. A grin that falls away as I reach Becca's doorway. Her dad's out, and Becca is sleeping. I sigh and turn away, let down.

"Hey there," someone hisses.

I glance back into the room, uncertain where the voice is coming from. Becca's eyes are slits. "Hey?"

"Come on in," she says. I do, and the hint of a smile creases one of her cheeks. "I've been pretending to sleep."

"You are a great actor."

I sit beside her. The bed is raised higher than usual, and she glances down at me.

"They raise it for sponge baths," she says.

"And you want me to—"

"Uh, no, I'm only saying it's so the nurse doesn't have to bend."

"Why are we whispering?" I ask.

"I don't want to talk to people."

"You're talking to me."

"You're different."

We lapse into silence for a second. "Why don't you want to talk to people?"

From the corner of one eye, a tear makes a break for it across her temple. "That's why."

"Sorry." She doesn't want to talk for fear she'll cry, but I'm not sure what I can say. Her father did explain that the steroids cause mood swings.

"I'm sorry. I'm scared," she says.

"But the biopsy is done, right? If not, I can bring my headset again. I left it at home so my parents could use it."

"It's not the procedure," she replies, eyes still shut. "I'm worried I won't get life right."

"You've done awesome so far," I say, waving an arm at the wall. "Your art. Your—"

"Can you go to a party and dance, or bang on some drums, or hop on a bike and go to a friend's house just because?"

I laugh. "You make it sound so hard."

"I'm serious. Those things *are* hard for me. When I was learning to play the piano, my parents wouldn't let me play Bach. Said it was too *vigorous*."

I keep forgetting how sheltered a life she's led.

"This is the end game for me," she says. "I've got no more excuses."

"Well, yeah, but it's also the start, right?" I reach up and grip her hand, and I tense when she threads her fingers with mine.

"I've always known I had a heart defect, but the problems really started when I was nine. I had arrhythmia—atrial fibrillation. Basically, my heart went nuts. Two hundred forty beats a minute, and it wouldn't slow down."

With her hand beneath her gown, she makes the fabric flutter. It reminds me of a sparrow having a bath. "I could watch it, just like this. I was so scared. But the doctors explained that they could put in a pacemaker. So we did. I wasn't scared anymore."

"Well, that's good." I'm distracted by the feeling of her finger stroking the back of my hand.

"For a while, yeah, but I still had problems, so a

couple of years later, they had to give me an ablation. That's where they fry some circuits on your heart to stop it from beating when it shouldn't. Another surgery. More school missed. Time. A couple of years after that, I needed a new type of pacemaker—four leads, four wires, another surgery. Every time I started to decline, we had options. Solutions. I wasn't scared."

"But then you got a new heart."

"Not quite. The doctors here are pretty good at keeping me alive. After I went into heart failure, they put in an LVAD—a left ventricular assist device. They plug in half an artificial heart that does the pumping for me. I had a backpack with a battery I had to keep charged."

"Whoa." Now I understand what she meant when she said about wanting to feel unchained.

"Yeah, pretty bad, huh?"

"I sometimes forget to brush my teeth."

"You're right, same same." She grips my hand. "Did you forget today?"

"My teeth?" I raise an eyebrow. "No."

"Good, good," she says almost to herself. "Well, I never forgot to charge. But it was like shackles. Couldn't do anything, not that I felt like doing anything. Climbing stairs was challenge enough."

"But I don't understand. Now you have a heart, so why are you scared?"

Her eyes water, but she nods. "If this doesn't work—" She pauses. "If this doesn't work, there might not be another one, or I might never qualify for another one.

They only last fifteen years on average. Did you know that?"

I shake my head. "No."

Another tear.

"Becca, you know, in a way you're just like the rest of us."

She stares at me, confused.

"Yeah, you're just a girl with a heart. You could get cancer. You could be hit by a car. We all live with these fears."

"Just a girl with a heart, huh? Fifteen years on average, remember?" She touches her chest. "As for cancer, these drugs increase my chances by a lot."

"So you're a little different. You going to let that stop you?"

"You sound like a friend of mine." She blinks away another tear and smiles. "He dared me to do something."

"Really. And what was the dare?"

"It's a favor I'd like to ask." We're whispering again, and her grip is so tight.

"Yeah."

"Will you take off your makeup for me?"

I frown. "Your friend dared you to ask me to take off my makeup?"

She chuckles. "No, but I want to see your real face when I ask you."

I hesitate.

"Come on, this is so the most embarrassing thing I've ever done."

But Becca doesn't realize what she's asking me to do. I'll need to sneak out of here without being seen. But I think I know where this is headed. My heart seems to trip over itself, and I wonder what else arrhythmia could be a symptom of. "Okay." I release her hand, missing her touch already.

At her sink, I use a towel to scrape off the makeup and then wash my face with warm, soapy water. When I'm done, I turn.

"Not bad. Now come over here," Becca says. "Hurry—my dad will be back soon." She uses the buttons on the side of the bed to raise her back and lower the whole thing at the same time.

For a moment we listen to each other breathe.

"Will you kiss me?" she asks. "I've never really kissed anyone."

I hesitate. "Me?" I glance to the door, feeling exposed. An imposter.

"Don't be an idiot." She rolls her eyes, and her expression swings from expectation to annoyance.

"It isn't just the steroids talking?" I blurt.

"What? No!" The bed begins rising again. "It's okay. Forget about it."

"No, no, I just don't want you to regret...it being with me."

"You're cute and all, but you're right, it's not like I'm in love with you or anything."

"I'll do it." I step closer.

She's shaking her head, the bed still rising. "I don't want a pity kiss."

"Do you want a kiss or what?" I press close and smell her. Beneath the antiseptic smell, the caustic detergent used on the sheets and the strange basil aroma of her hair, there's another scent—oil pastels and orange lip gloss.

"Not anymore," she says and turns to face the wall.

"I'll kiss you," I say.

"And then I'll hit the nurse call button."

"Only if you *want* a kiss! You asked me." She says nothing. Her shoulders begin to shake. "Are you crying? Why are you crying?"

"I rescind kissing consent."

"I'm sorry."

She rolls around to face me, eyes shimmering, lips full, face hot, and she's the most beautiful girl I've ever seen, and I want to kiss her as much as I've ever wanted anything, and I lean in, gently turning my head as I do.

"My heart is rejecting," she whispers when I'm close. "That's why I'm crying."

THIRTY-FOUR

I stumble, hit the IV stand and then grip it for balance. "What did you say?" I ask, heat rushing through me.

"My heart is rejecting."

The first sound from my throat isn't quite human.

"No, it can't be. Not for sure, right?" She gives me this odd look, as if to say, *It's my heart that's rejecting, not yours. But she's wrong.*

"The biopsy results came back. The numbers are bad." Her hands are tight balls in her lap. I glance at the heart monitor, which shows Minnie's heart still beating ninety-seven times per minute.

"But that's not possible," I say. "Are the doctors doing everything they can?"

"They're pumping me full of immunosuppressants and steroids—everything they've got."

Just then a doctor walks in. It's the tired one from the staff room. The one with the pot of coffee. His gaze travels from Becca's face, wet with tears, to my outfit and my anger. "What's up, Becca?" he asks carefully.

This is like my experience with Minnie all over again. *There's nothing we can do. She's already gone.*

No!

"Are you her doctor?" I ask, struggling to hold back the fear and rage welling in me.

Again he glances to Becca. "Her surgeon. What's the concern?"

"Nothing," Becca says. "Dappy here was just leaving."

My pulse races. This isn't the end. "Becca says she's rejecting, but that's not possible. It's too early to know, right? There's other stuff you can do, right? Just need to get the right balance of drugs." I hear Becca's fears come through my mouth and understand. There are no more solutions. Her drawings. Her diorama of herself protecting a magical stone from encroaching demons. It all makes sense.

The doctor cocks his head, moving slowly to grip me by the elbow. "It's okay for Rebecca to share the details of her care with you, but I can't." He's guiding me out, but I resist. When I glance over my shoulder, Becca has turned her head back to the wall. She asked to kiss me just moments ago. What is happening? *My heart is rejecting.*

The doctor manages to deposit me in the doorway.

"But—"

His hand moves to grip my shoulder. "We're doing the best we can."

They don't understand who Becca is to me. The heart of my sister. It's all I have left of Minnie. "Then try harder!" The shout rings out. Footsteps stop. Doors open. My voice drops. "You *have* to save her."

From the bed Becca shouts, "That doctor you're screaming at saved my life at least half a dozen times! That doctor is probably the most important person in my life. Get out of here!"

A steady click of heels down the hall. "What seems to be the issue…" Dr. Lebow's voice trails off as she stares at me. Dappy without his makeup. Recognition flashes. "*You*," she says.

This is the doctor I threatened to kill. This is the doctor who presided over the death of my twin sister.

"Please save her," I say.

Dr. Lebow begins to speak, then stops. After a moment she points at me and says, "Because of all the joy you have brought people over the last few weeks, I will give you fifteen minutes to leave this unit, return the outfit and exit the hospital premises. In fifteen minutes I *will* call security. If you are seen here again, you will be arrested for trespassing and anything else I can come up with. Do you understand?"

"I was only—"

"Do you understand?" she says again, louder and more firmly.

"Yes, ma'am."

She checks her watch. "Go."

I glance back toward Becca. She has her earbuds in, eyes shut as she cries. I sag, tears streaming down my face. I leave. Part of me wants her to know who I really am—it might change something. She might call me back. But she doesn't know me.

Everyone stares as I leave the unit and the waiting room. It could be that they heard it all. I'm ashamed. In the volunteer office, Fatima watches grimly as I pull off the shoes, the pants and the shirt. Then she holds the door open for me as I head for the lobby. I sense the eyes of security guards. I don't know what else to do. The revolving doors thud with the passage of each person as they exit. Accelerating and then decelerating sharply. Thud, thud, thud…thud…thud. Thud, thud, thud…thud…thud. Once through those doors I'm never allowed back.

I text Dennis a string of messages.

They caught me.

I'm banned.

Becca doesn't want to see me but doesn't even know who I am. Her heart is rejecting.

What do I do?

Dennis responds, first with a sad-face emoji and then: Sorry, man. This is a puzzle I can't hack.

Puzzle. I pocket the phone after checking the time. Only five minutes have elapsed.

I need help. I know only one person who might be able to solve my predicament. Someone who loves a good puzzle.

Eight minutes remain.

"I need to speak to Joy," I tell Jeannie. She squints at me. "It's me, Dappy, without the makeup." She nods with recognition and waves me through.

"Sure, but she's in a helluva mood. Room 358."

I knock at Joy's door. She's doing a crossword in the light of the windows. "What's a seven-letter word for 'go away'?" she asks without looking up.

"Vamoose. It's me, Dappy. Emerson. Emmitt, I mean."

She looks up. "What are you talking about?"

"I have"—I check my watch—"seven minutes before I get arrested. Can you help me?"

She sets aside the half-finished crossword. "Live-action escape room? I'm in."

"Here's the situation. My sister, Minnie, died. She gave her organs away, and I hunted down everyone who received them to film them, so my parents could see all the good Minnie did."

"Odd, but I'm following so far. Go on," Joy says. "Sorry, BTW."

Six minutes.

"Thanks. My heart—the person who received my sister's heart, she didn't want to talk to me, so I hacked the hospital records to figure out who she was and found out she was still in the hospital. Because they sort of caught me during the whole hacking thing, I had to disguise myself as a clown to sneak onto her unit, where I tried to meet her and help her. We were already talking in letters, and I sort of really—"

"Like her, yup, go on," she says.

"We made the video, but she still doesn't know who I am. I just found out her heart—my sister's heart—is rejecting, and I went ballistic, and the doctor figured out who I am, and she sent me away and security is going to arrest me if I don't leave the hospital in six—no—five minutes."

Joy's face has lost its hardness. Her lower lip protrudes, and her head tilts. She rises and reaches for my hand. I hit her halfway across the floor in a big hug.

"That sucks. What a mess," she says.

I'm crying again. But I don't have time for tears. "How do I fix this? How do I tell her how I feel and that I'm sorry? I only wanted to help everyone."

A wet splotch of tears darkens the shoulder of her gown. Joy's shaking her head as if I'm asking all the wrong questions. "You can't help anyone from a jail cell," she says. "You can't help everyone. You have to go, but before you do, I have a riddle for you."

"Can't you just give me the answer?"

"No, I don't think so. I don't think you'll make it out of here if I do."

I nod.

"What, when divided by eight, can create eight more, but adding the eight will never be whole?"

Three minutes. I frown, trying to force myself to think. Blood pounds in my ears.

"Go!" she cries.

I run. Past the penguin. Past Jeannie. Down the stairs and out the atrium doors even as security files in behind me.

Outside I find a spot near a large oak tree. Shaking, I repack my bag and draw deep, shuddering breaths.

Finally I sit down, press my back against the rough bark and sob. I cry for Becca. I cry for Minnie. I cry for the struggling heart they share. And I can't seem to stop. I have no answer, no solution to Joy's riddle, no way to fix anything. Like Becca, I am out of options. The person I need to talk to about it all is gone. I press my palms against my eyes and still my tears.

It's as though I'm holding my breath, but it's not breath I'm holding, it's misery, weighing me down, slowing my motions, as I stumble for the subway. As the doors open at my station platform, so do the gates to my pain. Becca had tethered me to Minnie. And finding Becca was meant to be a way to heal my family. The only way out, my film, has failed.

I push out of the subway car, ignoring other passengers, and climb the steps to the street, forcing my leaden legs on. I push through into the cool hall of home and right into my bed, where I fold myself into a fetal position, under my covers, the lightsaber of my Star Wars blanket at my throat.

THIRTY-FIVE

The empty walls of my room echo my gloom. I bury my head under the covers, entering a rank, unwashed underworld. People shift in and out of the room. I'm sat up and leaned forward. Mugs of soup are pressed against my lips. I only ever taste salt. Tears. Broth. Tears and broth.

Letters are read to me by my father. Then by my mother. She cries too.

Dennis cuts into my eyeline, but I focus on nothing. He's a blur.

"She's listening to death metal," he says. "She's drawing again—Dark Heart—it's not good, Emmitt, all twisted corpses riding zombie dragons and…" *Blah, blah, blah.* A stifled blur. Someone opens a box. A poster is unfurled.

Eileen arrives. An hour later, a day? I have no idea. For a few minutes she uses the headset. She faces my mother, who grips her stomach with both hands as she speaks with Eileen. They argue, but finally Eileen squats by my bedside and asks how she can help. Then Gerry shows up with an iPad, swiping through what are probably photos of rare moths or butterflies, if I care to see. I don't. He fades out of view but exclaims over Minnie's diorama. When he returns, he holds the picture from the shelf and smiles sadly.

"That looks like a good day," he tells me.

"It was," my dad says.

It was. A nail is hammered into the wall.

"School," someone says eventually. "You don't want to miss the start of eleventh grade."

"I don't really want anything," I explain. On the first day of school, Minnie and I would decide what to wear together. Every first day. Together. So many firsts after a death.

Words at least please them, and they go away.

For a while.

My mother keeps repeating something. On the fifth repetition, I hear, "Rebecca wants the end of the story." In my gut I know she doesn't. *Is she Shelagh? Stabbed by needles, a cat originally with nine lives and seven heads, but only one left now.* With a diving skunk, and Ivan as bait, the story can't end well. Besides, she doesn't want the ending from Dappy. Only from her heart brother. And he only wants to sink and sink.

Eileen returns. My mother speaks with her again. They're no longer fighting.

I sleep and wake. Sleep and wake. There's no rhyme or reason, but I prefer sleeping. I go to pee, eyes half-open, my hand brushing one wall to keep me upright. But on my return, I crawl under covers that feel different.

Grandmother's quilt perhaps. I dream. And forget.

When I wake, Ivan watches the diving skunk. The skunk's beady stare fixes on the vole. This is the end. Ivan has invited the crowds to watch, so that they will see in his sacrifice what they have wrought. But that won't bring Ivan back.

And then I realize I'm in Minnie's room. In her bed. Crying on her pillow. My mother stands in the center of the room. She looks herself. Her before-Minnie-died self.

"Mom," I say. "You're back."

She comes to me, sits on the bed and leans over, running a hand over my forehead. This close, I can see veins running blue beneath her pale skin. She quivers like a leaf. Eyes on me, she says, "You need to get up, Emmitt."

I close my eyes and relax into the tender raking of her fingers through my hair.

"I'm sorry," she whispers.

I keep my eyes shut. Eyelids like walls.

"I'm so sorry for abandoning you. You must have felt so alone. So scared."

Yes.

"So...angry."

I feel my Adam's apple bob. *Yes!* A tear sneaks between my eyelids and slides into the hair at my temples.

"To have implied that we wished you hadn't been born. That's a terrible thing. I'm so, so sorry."

I nod. "It's okay."

"It's not." After another moment of silence, during which the world slides a fraction more into balance, she adds, "You have an email."

I blink away the tears. She hands me my phone and an open email.

> *I may not be able to write much more. Nothing bad. Just think it'll be good for me to move on with this wonderful life, you know? Maybe you've already come to this conclusion too. That this is unnatural and unhealthy.*
> *I guess it's why you've gone quiet.*

She doesn't know...

> *The clown came a few days ago, and I tried, I swear I really tried, to kiss him, but things became awkward. His eyes told me it was more than a kiss, and that made me think I should wait for the right guy. I'm sorry it can't be you, but I have my reasons.*

Rejecting.

> *I will do it though. I will.*
> *I promise to take good care of your sister's heart. Before I go, I have one thing to ask. Could you finish the* Ivan the Vole *story? I want something for Shelagh too. Don't leave her in the dark. What's the twist? I can't figure it out.*
> *I love you.*

Becca blooms in my mind, all pastels and lip gloss. She didn't sign it.

I slip back under the covers into my underworld, where I am safe with her. The door opens and closes.

I sleep. And wake. At some point I move back to my room, collect my virtual-reality gear and join Minnie at the campfire, swearing to myself it'll be the last time I do this, but after the final strum on her guitar—each time—I hit *play* again. I can visit Becca the same way whenever I like. Maybe that's all I need.

"Liver Brother!" Joey shouts. "My turn!"

Joey yanks the blanket off the bed.

"Why do you deserve your organs if this is how you intend to treat them? Huh?"

I shudder in a ball, but he doesn't go away.

"One *week* you've been sleeping. Get the hell up. It's the one-week anniversary of my last drink. No thanks to you, I might add." Joey kneels on the side of the bed. I feel the mattress bend. "The first night you didn't call, I figured you were testing me, and I took the challenge—didn't touch a drop. But the second night...*that* was hard. You'd left me to the bottle. Hard. But my kids and me, we three ferrets watched some of my favorite movies, and I pushed through it. The third night I was pissed at you. Real mad. You *abandoned* me. You broke a promise. And I know you've watched *The Godfather* enough to know what that means to us Italians. Well, now I'm even more pissed. Your friend Dennis called me, told me what had happened, and I thought, What a goddamn hypocrite."

He leaves the bed. My mattress springs groan, and light fills the room. "At least when I was drinking, I felt like I was accomplishing something. What can you do from bed?"

In the corner of the room, my mom looks uncomfortable. Her hair has a brushed-out gloss to it. Although tired and lined, her cheeks have color, and her eyes are alive and in focus.

"Why do you want to live?" Joey asks, and I recognize the question.

I bring people stories. I bring people into stories.

"Why are *you* worth saving?"

I see now how harsh a question this is. I'm not sure I can live up to this standard every day. *I will give it my all.*

"How will sleeping more help you?"

Am I addicted to sleeping? "I'm not sleeping. I'm being sad. *Sadness is tractable.*"

"Emmitt, your heart sister isn't Minnie. All of us together. We're not Minnie."

What, when divided by eight, can create eight more, but adding all eight will never be whole? Joy said I couldn't handle the answer, but I can now. An organ donor. A donor's organs can save eight people. But you can't put them back together again to replace the person who was lost. Joy saw right through it all. My movie had never been about my parents. It was always for me, to bring Minnie back to me. This was about me facing my grief, which was why I couldn't face Becca's heart's rejection. But the video worked, just not how I had imagined it. It brought everyone here, and there my mom stands.

I say, my voice hoarse, "You're right."

"Well, we're not dead. Your family isn't dead."

My mom's biting on her knuckles—this is hard for her to hear, like it was for Carina.

"You aren't dead."

No. I'm not. *I'm sorry it wasn't me. I'm so sorry I wasn't there to catch you. I'm sorry I abandoned you in the hospital. That I couldn't think beyond myself to what you would have wanted.* Shame rushes through me. I taste bile.

"So what are you going to do?" Joey asks.

I bring people into stories.

I have an idea.

THIRTY-SIX

It's not a crazy idea. It's brilliant.

I explain the plan to Joey. When the nurse gathered the patient wish lists, Becca had asked for the view from the top of her roof. She'd gone on to explain in her letters that it wasn't the big adventures she missed. It was the little ones. Investigating the bakery alley. Sprinting down a hill. For my apology, I'll create a VR world for Becca of everything she always wanted to do but couldn't. Then I'll send my gear to the hospital, and at an appointed time we'll join each other in the VR world, where I'll reveal my real self to her—well, my virtual person, but really real.

"Really real?" Joey asks.

"As Emmitt," I say.

"It's crazy."

"Yeah."

"It could work."

All I need is my camera and tripod. No one in my family seems to care about my plan or even my decision to climb a roof—they're just happy that I'm up. After ushering Joey out of my room, I pull jeans over my underwear and a clean T-shirt over my head. Only then do I notice the changes to my room.

Books line the shelves. Posters dot the walls. A new picture hangs above my bed. It's of the ugliest moth I've ever seen, blown up a hundred times. Beneath it *Find the beautiful* is written in an elegant hand. My friends did this.

Something's missing though.

I push open the basement door and walk down the wooden steps. The box containing Minnie's raven sits behind the bin of Halloween decorations. My fingers trace the smooth, cool wood. I snap open the brass hasp to reveal the oily rainbow of the bird's feathers. Its eye follows me, and my chest tightens. I ease the lid closed and carry the raven up to my room. Burying my fingers in its soft ruff, wrist pressing against the cold metal of the clock, I lift the gift from the box and set it beside the diorama. I shift the raven left and right, trying to position it so its feathers catch light from the window, but its eyes flash, and I realize they're set with star sapphires.

I read the time on the clock and shudder—ten fifteen. It's the time Minnie was hit. The time of her death. Minnie's friends really are weird.

I owe Divina and Hal an apology. Maybe I can find a piece of her in them as well.

"Emmitt," my mom calls, and I tear myself from the raven's brilliant eyes.

"Emmitt, you need something to eat. Come sit," she says. But I'm already tromping down the hallway. "At least take something to go."

I turn and catch the plastic-wrapped sandwich she lobs at me. "It's good to see you off the couch, Mom."

"You too, Emmitt. Thank you for taking care of me and for forgiving me for not taking care of you." She holds my stare for a good five seconds before my eyes blur with tears. "I love you."

"You too, Mom." The "Mom" emerges as a croak. "I love you too." That feeling of invincibility in my gut like everyone has my back. That lightness in my head. These are symptoms of love.

Outside the air is thick with heat. My jeans cling to my legs, and I've only been walking a minute. But I have no time to waste. Becca has waited long enough. If her heart is rejecting, I will jam her remaining time full of living.

I pull Becca's address from the photo of her medical record. Then I delete any trace of those pictures. I was wrong to have hacked the hospital, wrong to have betrayed the trust of my heart family. I will make reparations.

Between the subway, the train and the walk, it's a two-hour commute to her house, but that gives me time to figure out the technical aspects of my plan. I bring Dennis in on the strategy and ask him to rent me a second VR headset compatible with my own, and then I consider what it is I plan to film, rereading her letters and emails to me.

I need Becca to know that her heart brother and Dappy the Clown are one and the same. I want her to know me, and I need to apologize at the same time. An apology for believing I had the right to enter her life without her knowledge. I know why she didn't want to meet her heart family. Rejection doesn't occur overnight. *I don't want to meet you. I have my reasons.* She never left the PICU. She's been rejecting Minnie's heart all this time. It was guilt. I need her to know that it's okay.

At the bottom of the escarpment near where Becca lives runs a long trail that hugs the side of the cliff all the way to the top. It doesn't wind. It just climbs up. We will begin here. To climb this had been her definition of an awesome day. I turn on the camera and step in front of it.

"Hi, Becca. My name is Emmitt Highland, aka your heart brother, aka Dappy the Clown. Yes, we're the same person. I'm sorry I did what I did. I was trying to put my sister back together again. I was looking for her in the people who still hold a piece of her. Instead I found these amazing, different people who have survived so much, taught me so much.

"I am ready to accept my sister's death. You don't have to meet me ever again, but I hope we will. You see, while trying to find Minnie again, I found you. I don't want to lose that.

"I want to leave you with a gift. Something I hope you will one day do for real. Remember what you wrote when you were asked where you'd go if you could go anywhere? You said you didn't want to appear at the top of Everest. You wanted to know what it was like in the alley beside the bakery, to run down a hill at full speed or sit on the roof of your house. Well, today your wishes come true."

I point up the slope of the escarpment. "You also said that the power in the view from the mountaintop is from the climb. So let's go!"

I heft the tripod and, keeping it as steady as possible, begin the long run up the side of the escarpment. I start out hard, but the cliffs have trapped the heat and smog of the city, and I'm soon gasping and have to slow to a walk. Halfway up I enter a wooded area where it's cooler, and I pick up the pace. "There are benefits to teleportation," I say to the camera, lungs heaving, and keep climbing. The air clears of smog, and the sun shines as I trudge the final steps to the summit and gaze out over the city and beyond to the lake.

"Now the fun part," I say, drawing a great breath and releasing it slowly.

I turn to face the downward slope and begin to jog. The jog becomes a trot and then, after a particularly steep bit, a run. I study the path, feet dodging roots and stones. I'm not a runner, and the trip up the hill with all the gear was already painful. Muscle fibers in my thighs snap and twang as I pound down the hill, gaining more speed until my vision joggles with the camera, and I lift my chin to the sky and yell. I run all the way, through the cool woods and baking-hot open bits, back down into the hazy smog, wheezing, free arm windmilling, until I'm laughing at the bottom.

"Next," I pant, "the alley."

And I shut the camera off.

The evening shadows whisk some of my sweat away. Already my quadriceps ache, making it hard to walk down the hill to Becca's neighborhood. I don't know which bakery or which alley Becca meant in her comments, only the general area. A quick search on my phone isolates the main street with stores within walking distance of her home. I wonder why she never walked down an alley if she was so interested in it. The first bakery I pass has stores on either side, no alley, but the second explains everything. The alley isn't so much an alley as it is a "dark heart," a tunnel running the length of the bakery and the neighboring motorcycle-parts store.

I set up the tripod again. The alley smells pungent, and I gag once.

I wave a hand over my nose and hit *record*. "Really? This alley? This isn't an alley, it's a cave. A dungeon." I blow out a sigh and shake my head. "We may not make it out of here."

Picking up the tripod and camera, I shuffle into the alley-cave. Something drags across my scalp. I retch once before controlling my stomach. The end of the alley swirls in darkness, and I wonder what it would be like in daylight, thinking perhaps this part of the film can wait, but then I remember that Becca's heart is rejecting. My foot squishes on something, and I pull out my phone to use the flashlight function, then decide I don't really want to know what I stepped in.

A scratching echoes from the alley's end. "Geez, I don't really recommend this."

I finally get the flashlight function to work. The dead end of the alley materializes.

Two doors, each with seams but no handles, are on either side of the corridor. A painted brick wall and a mouse scratching at the door. A rat trap nearby.

"It's Ivan," I gasp. It's as if I'm the angel-skunk coming in for the kill. "This is our story. The ending. There's no escape, Ivan!"

I chuckle.

"What'll he do?" I ask. Ivan squints at me as if I'm the prey. "You know, your heart sister would open this rat trap and check for occupancy and then freshness. She brought ziplock bags with her everywhere she went, just in case. You have a brave heart. That's what you said you were missing, right? Courage? Well, now you have it in you."

Suddenly the door on the right opens. I cry out. So does the man with a hairnet, standing silhouetted against the light from the bakery. Ivan slips between the legs of the baker. The baker takes a look at me, shakes his head and drops a bag of garbage in the alley. The door shuts. Ivan is free for another day. Something slides between my legs, and I jump. It races into the corner, and I follow the sound with my flashlight to see what it is. A cat.

"Shelagh! A one-headed cat." She's made it out of the shadows after all.

I laugh. "That's it," I say. "The watching mice, seeing the truth, with Ivan in the jaws of the skunk, pull their needles and attack the skunk, but it's not enough. Shelagh pounces from the shadows to sink her claws into him. Together the mice and Shelagh save Ivan and chase the skunk away for good. Ivan is granted the boon of..."

I can still smell the freshly baked bread over the stench of garbage. "...a lifetime supply of day-old chocolate croissants."

I scan the rear wall with my flashlight. Someone has graffitied the brick to make it look three-dimensional, like the alley continues until it hits a white beach and a crystal-blue ocean. A man and a woman peer from either side of the exit, beckoning. This is pretty cool, even with the bag of garbage and the rat trap. Sometimes the end doesn't really have to be a brick wall.

"Next, your rooftop," I say, and I shut the camera off.

With gathering cloud cover, the street is almost as dark as the alley was. I have one more scene to film.

Something I hadn't considered until I near Becca's home is that people who want to see the view from their rooftop do not live in bungalows. Becca's house towers up three stories, looking out over a busy road that climbs the escarpment through a rock cut. The house's location on the hill makes it seem even taller. Cars rattle up the road, but few people walk here. I'm in luck, because the rear yard backs onto a school parking lot, and the building code has required a fire escape for the third story of the house. From the parking lot I peer up at the roof. If I'm standing on the railing of the fire escape, I should be able to swing my leg over the edge of the roof. My quadriceps ache just thinking about it. There's a dormer at that point, which I may be able to shimmy up. *Should. May.* This is stupid.

"Here we are," I whisper at the back gate to Becca's house, camera recording. "We're doing this."

Even *I* know this is dumb.

I reach over the gate to unlatch it, slip into the yard and close the gate behind me. I breathe. Between the noise of passing cars, I pick out the sound of water falling. A gazebo strangled with wisteria stands between me and a small pond populated with orange fish and the source of rushing water. The window facing the backyard is dark. A dog barks and barks. I can't stop sweating. I swipe greasy hands on my jeans.

The black iron fire escape is still warm from the sun. Against the green-painted brick, my white T-shirt will stand out. I scramble up the short ladder to the second story, passing a frosted window—probably a bathroom—and then on to the third floor. No matter how softly I step, the metal rings out beneath my sneakers. My legs burn from the running. This window has curtains and a steady blue light like that of a computer screen. I listen for evidence of my detection. *Nothing but the dog.*

I hold my thumb up to one of the camera lenses— so far, so good—and then heave myself onto the railing, balancing with a hand against the brick. Heights have never bothered me, but the narrowness of the rail does. It presses at my feet beneath the rubber soles of my shoes. The railing trembles. With my free hand, I swing the gear onto the roof, wedging a tripod foot into a leaf-jammed gutter. The tripod rolls a couple of times before stopping. When I stretch to get it, it is out of reach. I'm committed.

I lift a leg, and only my toes touch the edge of the gutter. My hamstring twinges in protest, the railing wobbling. I should have done this first and the run second. The flat-roof dormer will work as a ledge. But I'll have to jump and pull myself up in a single motion. It's that or… or tumble to the ground from three stories. Or I could leave my camera and come back with a hook of some sort to grab it—*this is ridiculous.*

But I don't have a rejecting heart.

I heave.

There's a moment when I'm not sure I'll make it. Asphalt shingle scrapes across my face. The gutter presses into my hips, bending and squeaking as I wriggle. My knee finds the gutter, which creaks as I strain to pull myself up. Wet leaves soak through denim. And then I'm on the roof.

I give my fist a silent pump. I made it.

Climbing the rest of the way to the ridge will be easier. I stay low, using the valley between the dormer and roof for stability, shifting the camera and tripod with me. The soles of my shoes rasp against the rooftop as I take small, careful steps. Finally my fingers curl over the peak, and I allow myself to straighten. I'm on top.

Suddenly a figure leaps up from their hiding spot, grinning madly. I startle and cry out. I fall backward, back and head slamming into the shingles, feet launching into the air as I roll. A hand snatches at my ankle and catches it, holding, keeping me from flipping and sliding off the roof. I stare up at a cloudy evening sky but still see stars.

Becca laughs. "I thought you'd never make it."

THIRTY-SEVEN

Becca has my shirt twisted in her grip even as we lie flat against the roof. I've spun around so that blood no longer rushes to my head, but I'm not yet ready to pry myself from the coarse shingles.

"I can't believe you did that," I say. "I almost died."

"I saved your life. Your friend told me you were coming," she says. Despite the heat emanating from the roof, she shudders with cold. "I've been waiting an hour. That gave me too much time to come up with crazy ideas."

"My friend?"

"Yeah, Dennis? He told me parts. He said you needed a bit less virtual reality."

A good friend.

"Like you need a bit more of it?"

"We balance each other."

"The hospital let you out? You're home?"

Becca swallows. "For now. My last kitten rampage

went better. My rejection numbers, I mean. Not great, but better."

Kitten rampage. Another heart biopsy.

"So you know who I am?" I ask. "You're not angry at me?"

"Deep down I suspected, but with everything else, my brain just didn't go there." She looks away. "Why'd you do it?"

"I wanted my sister back," I say. "She's me."

"And now?"

"I still want her back. I also know that she's gone, and I'm still here. But less."

Her stare is hot like the shingles.

"You were close." She shifts a fraction toward me. It's minute, but I notice the bare skin of her leg brush against mine.

"The closest."

"Willing to hack a hospital for her. To become a clown for her."

"The clown was for you," I say. "I am sorry."

She leans over, hip digging into my hip. "I don't have time for anger."

There's a moment when her heart beats against my chest, and I clench my eyes in a mixture of pleasure and pain. Becca drops back to the shingles with a sigh.

"It's not your fault," I say. "The rejection."

"I know," she replies. "I think I'm afraid to let go of dying Becca. Healthy Becca will have to think beyond weeks. Maybe I won't have to."

"Don't say—"

"Can we talk about something else?"

Tears fill her eyes.

"You're sad," I say. "Scared."

She nods.

It's this elephant in the room. On the house. "Your heart is rejecting. And that means you could die. That's really scary. Losing the rest of your life. A life that could be amazing."

Becca's started sniffling, unable to look my way yet unable to move.

So I continue, speaking the unspoken. "And there's nothing anyone can do, is there? That must feel so lonely."

She chokes as she nods. "So lonely."

"I'm sorry." I hold her. "Can I be a part of what's left?"

Her eyes squeeze shut. We let time and road noise roll over the question until it's gone.

"How'd you climb up here?" I ask.

"I'm stronger than I look." She shows me a rope ladder. "It's for emergency exits out of windows, but the principles are the same for going up."

"You could have left it there."

"And miss the chance to scare you?"

"I nearly fell."

"I had you." Her voice drops away along with her gaze.

"Let's see this view you've been going on about." I carefully edge up the roof to swing my legs over the ridge so that I'm sitting. Becca does the same, and then we're both facing the street. The lights of the city already shine with moist fairy rings, and the black waters of the lake shimmer with the last of the evening light.

"Is it everything you imagined?" I ask.

Her hand edges over top of mine. "Better."

"You said it's the climb that makes it worthwhile," I say.

"I was wrong. It's the company."

Over the week since I last saw her, some of the swelling in her face has gone down, revealing cheekbones and dimples.

"If we're going to keep this up, you're going to have to stop calling me Heart Sister."

Something in me. A spasm of pain. It releases and flutters away.

"I stopped long ago. You just didn't notice."

I lean in and hover at her lips.

"Are you really sure?" she whispers. "Because I don't know what comes next."

"Don't worry. It ends well for Ivan and Shelagh."

"Does it?"

"Yeah, in the alley. I'll explain later."

"I meant about my heart."

"No one knows what comes next." I thread my fingers through hers and stare long enough into her eyes that my mind tells me to look away, but I don't. I won't. "Like my sister, I'll love you for however long you have."

"Like your sister."

"Yeah, but unlike her, I'm going to kiss you."

"Are you?" She laughs.

"Subject to your consent."

Her chin juts. Her eyes close. And her mouth whispers, "Yes."

Our lips touch. I shut my eyes and focus on the sensation.

It's a bit...dry.

"So that's it?" she says, pulling away.

"Huh." That was *not* how I was expecting that to go. I am at a loss for words. But then I start to laugh. "Have you ever seen the movie *Back to the Future*?" I ask her. "The one where a crazy scientist builds a time machine out of a DeLorean?"

"Okay, that's pretty random," Becca replies. "Yeah, I've seen it. Why?"

"Well, you know the scene where Marty is trapped in a car with his mother, and she's trying to kiss him?"

"Wait a minute, are you saying I'm the *mother*?" Becca jabs me in the ribs.

"In this case, *sister*!" Oh god. Have I just ruined everything?

Becca is silent for a moment. Then she cries, "*Marty!*" in a perfect impression of Doc Brown.

Now we are both laughing so hard I'm afraid Becca will slide off the roof ridge. I put my arms around her, like I put them around Minnie, so many times. "Heart sister," I say.

"I can live with that," she whispers.

"You want to give it another shot?" I ask.

She fake gags, but she's smiling. "No, I'm good."

She snuggles in to me and we turn and watch the lights flick on below us. For the first time in a long while, I feel like everything is going to be all right.

EPILOGUE

One year following the brain death of my sister, I spot a letter from the National Transplant Organization in our mailbox. I pull it out, wave to our neighbor and go back inside, shutting the door on a muggy-for-July morning.

"Hey, Mom, they want to give Minnie a medal," I call.

She barks a laugh from the kitchen. "We can hang it around Lenore."

I didn't choose the name of Minnie's raven. I thought Poe was too bleak and preferred Memory, the name of one of Odin's ravens. But my mom's right. That's where the medal should go.

I read from the letter. "There's a ceremony for donor families. They're asking for photos." My mom has created a scrapbook. Apparently that's what accountants do to piece lives back together.

"Great," my dad says. "I'll bring vegetables shaped to look like—"

"Don't say it, Dad, seriously."

"What? What did you think I was going to say?" He's smiling. Not laughing yet, but smiling. We're doing better. Healing. The waves of sadness don't crash as frequently, and when they do, they don't pull us under. But the undercurrent remains near the surface.

Picking up a medal for Minnie sounds to me like a great idea, but on the night of the ceremony, I'm suddenly hesitant. At my side stands Becca. A year into her transplant, she's still with us. On too high a dosage of immunosuppressants, but, as she says, it's better than dead. Each time she visits the hospital, she also takes my VR gear. After her biopsy and kitten rampage, she drops the gear off at Jeannie's desk. Pediatrics is pretty good at setting it up on their own. Becca once asked after Joy on my behalf, but all the nurse would offer was a cryptic, "Joy escaped before the glass emptied." I wish I could see her again, but...well...privacy.

"Come on." Becca squeezes my fingers and pulls me inside the university auditorium where the presentation is being held.

The space is crowded with families. Big ones with dozens of people and all generations. Little ones like ours. People hold all manner of photo albums and scrapbooks, sharing photos and stories. Loved ones clutched tight in their grips. Hundreds of people from all walks of life pack the small hall.

A tall woman with close-cropped hair breaks from the crowd. She grins mischievously at me, as if we're sharing a moment.

"I was hoping you would make it," she says. "Can you guess who I am?"

"Martha!" Becca exclaims.

"Rebecca, right?" Martha asks, and Becca nods.

They hug, and then Martha hugs me, planting a kiss on my cheek. Then we're in a group hug.

"It's wonderful to meet you," she says. "How *are* you?"

It's a loaded question usually, but today it's okay. "We're all right," I say.

"And Ivan?"

"Last spotted him full of chocolate croissants," I reply.

"How's the gang?"

I laugh at that. I went searching for my sister and found a gang. "Good." And they are. We meet every month. I am getting used to seeing Eileen joke with Gerry. Joey's found a new addiction—running. I invited Dennis to attend the event, but he said it wasn't for him. But we see each other a lot, since he's my manager at the coffee shop where we both work.

"Nice. Well, I have a lot more people to meet. I hope you enjoy the speaker." She winks.

I catch sight of my mother hugging another woman. Scores of people are in tears. As they cry, others tear up. The place seems on the edge of falling apart. I glance at Becca, and she wipes her eyes.

"You too?" I laugh, but my eyes fill at the same time.

On a large screen photos slide in and out, replacing each other. Baby pictures. Family pictures. Old women. Teenage boys. Cultural celebrations. Fishing, water skiing, swimming, sledding and canoeing. Victories. Adventures.

"These are heroes," says a nervous woman at the podium. "Each one." She motions at the slideshow. The room quiets.

"Each of you lost someone about a year ago. I didn't. Last year was one of the worst moments in your life, but for me it was one of the best." Her hands grip the front of the podium. "About a year ago I gained one of your friend's, lover's or family member's organs."

At a break in her voice, she stops. "I'm sorry. I'm nervous. You lost, so I could live. It's a terrible gift to have to give. But you didn't have to give it. You chose to without knowing me, and that makes it even more special.

"When I was in hospital and couldn't breathe, I almost gave up. Each day of the 342 days I was on the transplant list, I almost gave up. One thing kept me going. Each morning I asked the team for the numbers. They'd tell me, 'We had twenty new registrations yesterday.' Sometimes it would be as many as a hundred. All I needed was one. See, the numbers were the number of new registrations to the organ-donation registry. When each person registered, it was like the group that cared about me grew. It was one more person cheering for me—that's what it felt like. You saying, 'Come on! You can do it! One more day.' And the next day there would be more. So I kept on, for 342 days. And I lived. And I can't tell you how grateful I am."

She begins to cry, then composes herself.

"This past fall," she continues, "I had even more people cheering me. I participated in the World Transplant Games."

That's when Becca pokes me. "You're squeezing my hand really hard," she says, and then she sees my face. "Are you okay?"

My mom too has seen, and she shifts between people to reach me.

"She has Minnie's lungs," I reply. "My lung sister."

My mom gasps, and she leans in to whisper in my dad's ear, and we all press together.

"I participated in four events. I *ran*. I ran for me, but I also ran to honor my donor. And I ran to honor you. The medals I won are yours, and we're here to give each of you one today."

"She did it," I say.

Way to go, Minnie.

The woman steps away from the microphone, and Martha takes her place, holding a medal and a long list.

"You want to say hello?" Becca asks.

"No, I don't think so," I reply, and I sink to a chair, hemmed in by my loved ones, as Martha begins calling up representatives from donor families. "I'm going to be okay."

From my wallet I pull out the photos of Minnie. There are five now. Her four class pictures and a cropped photo of us cliff jumping, hand in hand, leaping into the blue waters, delirious grins on our faces. In the picture my shoulder is bare of tattoos. It isn't anymore. I've had my tattoo changed though. The skin's a bit scarred and discolored, a bit like life post Minnie, but the *Do Not Recycle* is gone. I had it changed to *Reuse*. I've registered to be an organ donor. I'm proud of this choice. I hope my name will never need to be looked up, but if it is, it's there and ready to help eight people beat their demons, find the courage to change, keep up to their dreams and have more good days.

Like this one.

ACKNOWLEDGMENTS

It was an honor to write this novel. When a book's subject matter includes another person's pain, it increases the responsibility of the writer. It was a challenge to balance storytelling with the knowledge that I drew story from the pain of others. I hope I did it justice. My deepest apologies if you feel I did not.

This book only moved forward due to the support of a lot of good people. Thank you, David Hartell and the Canadian National Transplant Research Program, Dr. Greg Knoll and Dr. Matthew-John Weiss for your technical expertise, support and many introductions. All errors are mine. Thank you, Larry McCloskey, Alma Fullerton, Nate Estabrooks, the Sunnyside Writers Group, the InkBots and the Odyssey Workshop 2016 alum—every book requires a supporting cast of authors. Caroline Pignat, thank you for such a spectacular blurb.

Thank you, Diane Craig, for sharing your story. Thank you to Ronnie Gavsie, Rabbi Bulka and all the people at Trillium Gift of Life Network, who showed me how much you do to improve the lives of others. And to Dr. Edward Hickey and the team at Toronto General Hospital that cared for my brother. You are lifesavers. High fives, fist bumps and eternal hugs.

Martin Stiff, Glendon Haddix, Catherine Adams, Jessica Holland and Deborah Dove, thank you, thank you, thank you! To my family, to Andrea and to my daughters for being first readers and always there for me.

My gratitude to the Orca pod: Tanya Trafford for your leveling up of, well, everything; Andrew Wooldridge for taking a chance; and the production and marketing team, without whom all our invested time means very little indeed, my gratitude.

I gratefully acknowledge the financial support of the City of Ottawa's Arts Funding Program. Money means time, and time allows for writing.

To my brother, Mark, who is in every word of this book, you've shown us all how to live well with a bum heart. You're even more amazing with a great heart.

Finally, to my brother's heart sister and her family, what can I possibly say? Thank you for your gift. It means life for a brother, a son, a husband and a father.

Your heart found a good home. I love you.

Michael F. Stewart is an award-winning author of many books for young people in various genres, including *Ray vs. the Meaning of Life*. He lives in Ottawa.